A HORSE
Like Mr. Ragman

A HORSE
Like Mr. Ragman

by RACHEL RIVERS-COFFEY

SCHOLASTIC BOOK SERVICES
NEW YORK · TORONTO · LONDON · AUCKLAND · SYDNEY · TOKYO

Cover photo by Yarvin,
from Frederic Lewis, Inc.

ISBN 0-590-31296-0

12 11 10 9 8 7 6 5 4 3 2 1   4   0 1 2 3 4 5/8

Printed in the U. S. A.   06

*for
Armfield
and Donna
and Tam*

Chapter One

I probably never really liked Eva. She was a blonde girl with bright blue eyes and more money than old Major could have jumped over in his best days. We got to the stable every morning about the same time, but certainly in different ways.

Eva arrived in a chauffeured limousine, her golden hair pulled up in curls on top of her head, her Ratcatcher shirt starched and pressed, her jodhpurs belted to her tiny waist, and her boots shined so you could see yourself in them.

She was usually impatient and had a habit of smacking a crop against her boot, and she rolled her eyes and hummed to herself. About that time, I'd arrive.

My "chauffeur" was my father, who had a habit of wearing his sleeves rolled up above his elbows and playing country music on the truck radio. The old door creaked and out I stepped, black hair pulled down in pigtails, my nose sunburned, shirt out at the waist, rolled-up dungarees, bobby socks, and sneakers. I wasn't as tall as Eva by two or three inches, but I was slimmer. If there were any earthshaking differences between us otherwise, they were noticeable only to Eva, not to the horses.

"Be good, Chicken," Dad would say, and Eva would almost fall over laughing.

"Chicken," she'd say between giggles.

"It's a family joke," I'd say.

Dad would drive off, his broken-down truck leaving a cloud of dust in the road. You could hear the music growing weaker and weaker, the horses stamping inside their stalls, birds playing chase in the treetops.

One morning Eva just couldn't resist saying, "Did you look like a chicken when you were little?"

"What do you think?" I said right back.

"Most likely," Eva said, getting tired of teasing me. I wasn't about to tell her why they nicknamed me Chicken. It was one of those family things that other people never understand.

"Shall I bring your horse, madame?" I said, and off I went to saddle and bridle Eva's lean, beautiful Thoroughbred. I was the groom and Eva was the rich lady, although we were both the same age — twelve — and about equal in riding ability.

You would think she was Queen of the Nile the way she strutted around, showing off all the time. Everybody else was dirt under her feet except Mrs. Nolly, owner of Nolly Stables. Mrs. Nolly's comment was, "I just don't pay any attention to spoiled people — or horses, for that matter. You shouldn't, either."

But the differences were so great that I couldn't help dwelling on them. While Eva was off riding in the park, I was forking out the stalls, rolling the wheelbarrow back and forth to the manure pile, and putting down fresh beds of straw.

While Eva McCormack was dreaming about her weekend, Elizabeth Mae Jiggsen — that's me — was currying and brushing horses; tickling their noses while the blacksmith, Carver Coy, did his work; and taking reservations over the phone while Mrs. Nolly went over her ledger and checked to see if any extra supplies were needed.

By ten o'clock, my hair was full of hayseed and my hands and face were grimy. Mrs. Nolly sent me to fetch grooming tools she'd left somewhere, and Carver Coy was forever misplacing his rasp. Every day was about the same, those summers in Blowing Rock. Anyone who hung out around the stable had better be prepared to do his share of the work.

But that wasn't the case with Eva. She was a *client*. She boarded her horse there, she worked him out every morning, and by ten o'clock she returned to the barn looking cool as a cucumber in a tossed salad.

She stepped down from the saddle, handed me the reins, and out of nowhere came the giant black limousine. Eva got in without so much as good-bye and was gone for another day.

There I was, standing beside the most perfect horse I had ever seen, the very horse I'd dreamed of having. But he wasn't mine — only mine to take care of. I'd groom him and cool him down, and then I'd see to his tack.

Eva had been told a hundred times not to canter him in Rock Creek. "It's full of stumps," Mrs. Nolly said. "It was good for building up the legs," she said, "but that was years ago." Of course, Eva spent most of her time galloping through Rock Creek with the result that her girth, stirrup straps, and reins had to be saddle-soaped and polished every morning. By me — Chicken Jiggsen.

4

I would have preferred spending all my time hanging over the stall door looking at her horse. The brass nameplate on his halter said GARRISON'S QUARTER, but we all called him William Tell. Because, as Mrs. Nolly said, "He has that astonished look about him, as if someone had just shot an apple off his head with a bow and arrow."

Once Mrs. Nolly named a horse, it stuck, and the minute she saw one, a name popped right into her head.

I sure wished she'd been around the day Dad looked down at me and dubbed me his "little Chicken." At her house, Eva was probably called Darling or Baby Doll — something more suited to her station in life. That was the way it went. Eva was terribly wealthy. I was not.

Dad worked very hard in his heating and plumbing business, and Mom took after her grandfather, Lucius Goins, the artist. She spent her time out on the screened-in porch, dabbing her oil paints onto canvases, and grumbling to herself when she made an error and had to start again.

I worked hard, learning all about horses and helping Mrs. Nolly teach her afternoon classes. Among our regular students were the Bledsoe twins who rode the sorrels, Prince and Peter, very well, but who usually looked like soft sleepy kittens even when riding at a canter. Mrs. Nolly did her best to make them look like serious competition, but to no avail.

And there was Suzanne, another rich girl spending the summer in the mountains near Blowing Rock, although Suzanne was more like a sister than a friend, and she didn't mind pitching in and working.

And there was Toby, with his mouth full of braces and his hands full of chocolate candy. He couldn't resist eating and, as a result, he was roly-poly fat. To make matters worse, his favorite horse was Stogy, a long, thin filly who only made him look fatter than he was.

And then there was Rusty Reinholt. He rode as though he'd been born on a horse. I loved watching him take the fences in the hunt field and noted that he looked just as good on the little Palomino, Jack, as on Beau's Bonnet.

"That boy can flat-out ride a horse," Mrs. Nolly said.

"Aye," said Carver Coy, leaning up against a locust tree, "he's a dandy. And I notice Elizabeth watches him awfully close, too."

I swelled up like a puff adder and said, "I don't either."

But I did.

Chapter Two

Late on the afternoon of that warm June day, we hit a lull when there was nothing pressing to be done. Carver was on the phone ordering additional grain and hay; Mrs. Nolly was out back scrubbing some soiled horse blankets; and it was time at last for me to get astride a horse.

After all, it had been the whole winter since I'd put my left foot into a stirrup and swung up into a saddle. Mrs. Nolly's personal mount, Big Boy's Major, was patient with me as I tried over and over to get the bridle on him. At seventeen hands height, he was the tallest, bulkiest horse in the barn, and at five feet, two inches height, I couldn't even reach his mouth, much less hope to get the headstall over his ears. Major couldn't be happier, but Mrs. Nolly guessed what was happening and yelled to Carver, who was just coming out of the tack room and into the corridor. "Help that child get a bridle on Major, or she'll be till tomorrow doing it."

Carver did help, putting on the saddle, too. Then he gave me a leg up and a little advice. "You've got to remember, now, the Major's older every year, and he hasn't got the tension of a young horse. So don't ride him too tight at the rein. And don't be stiff and uneasy just because of his bigness, now. This is Mrs. Nolly's prize possession, and you must use her golden rule and be kind about pulling on that steel bit. It could be the other way around, you know, and the bit be in *your* mouth, instead."

Chuckling, waving us away, Carver went over to the old rocker in front of the tack room to soak up a little sun. Of Mrs. Nolly's three Thoroughbreds, Major was the one she chose to ride and show herself. The barn boasted two other purebreds, a flashy eight-year-old called Beau's Bonnet, and a durable old hunter called, simply, King. Sometimes King was the horse I rode, but I often wound up showing equitation on any number of other horses.

They were all sound as a dollar, and to show off riding skills, it really didn't matter about the horse's breeding. But there were

8

other classes where it did matter, and if you were going to score high in the judges' notebook, you had to have just the right horse under you.

And, as Mrs. Nolly well knew, in my mind Major had always seemed the perfect horse, despite the fact he was far too large for a rider my size. I probably looked like the stem on top of a pumpkin when riding him, but I felt like I was entering the arena at Madison Square Garden. I felt like I could give Eva and her beautiful gelding some real competition, especially since Major and I were old friends, and I knew all his tricks.

Trick number one: He liked to pretend he'd never seen the gate to the riding ring and suddenly shied sideways. I stuck in the saddle and he flicked his ears back and forth in recognition of that fact. The Major might be older every year — who isn't? — but he wasn't any less smart.

He ambled into the ring, slung his head to ward off the flies, and took those long rolling steps that are difficult to sit after a long time of being on the ground. The black horse took the right-hand railing as he'd done a thousand times before and moved along on his giant steps and lazily switched his tail.

I pressed my heels down and back to align the stirrups with the girth. While a perfect fit for Mrs. Nolly, Major's saddle was big for me, and I tended to push my feet forward to compensate. The part where I'd really feel it was in keeping my knees tight to the forward-seat saddle. Muscles which hadn't been used since last fall went to work. Mrs. Nolly didn't believe in taking the easy way out. Riders at her stable had to ride on ice-slick leather, while other stables often provided a few jumping saddles with suede, easy-to-hold-to knee rolls.

Mrs. Nolly's attitude about that was, "If you can't stick to the saddle with your own two legs, I'm not going to buy outrageously expensive gear to convince a bunch of beginners they're better than they really are."

It was time for Major's second trick (I had to be thoroughly tested, you see). He merely pretended he'd never seen the concession stand before. Since the Horse Show Association owned the stable where he had lived every summer for the last ten years, he knew the faded plank building as well as he knew his tongue. However, he came to a stop, lifted his head, snorted in alarm with his ears pricked forward, and swung in a fast circle to the left, nearly losing me in the process.

Finally he wiggled his ears and settled down. I had passed. He was in pretty good hands, he figured. And speaking of hands, mine seemed clumsy on Mrs. Nolly's broad braided reins, but I took hold of them anyway and pushed Major into a steady, unswerving trot. He kept an amused eye to the rail as he passed the box seats and the grandstand and then the gate on which Carver now leaned, watching.

My elbows felt stiff; my hands were too high. There was a mile of daylight between my seat and the saddle when I posted. The fact was, I needed this little practice session a whole lot more than Major did. I was somewhat off balance and tended to lean too far forward from the waist up.

"Give yourself a little time to get back into it," Carver yelled. "Don't be so impatient. You'll be back to just as good as always. Relax!"

I did relax. My hands came down into position, although I still had my thumbs turned up like a novice. My elbows quit hugging my ribs, and as I straightened my back, I had more control at the trot. Major trotted on out, skimming over the ground, rounding the ring two more times before a nudge at his sensitive mouth told him to stop.

I had a bad habit of watching the ground when I rode, and that needed to be worked on. I was watching his shoulders to see which diagonal to post to, and when we went into the canter, I watched his shoulder to make sure he was leading with the correct front leg. When my riding legs "came back," I would be able to feel these subtle changes without looking down.

"Don't look down!" Carver yelled. He waved off my rough reintroduction to a horse's back, grinned comfortably, and went back to his rocking chair. I was loosening up very well by the time I pushed Major into a canter. He could cover more ground per stride than any other horse in the stable. His long, tapered legs glided along, the wind beat my hair back, the sun came down, and for a moment or two I pretended that Major was mine and we were smack-dab in the middle of the Highlands Charity Horse Show.

About that time, Major did trick number three, which consisted of his bucking as high as he could and taking off at a hard gallop. There was still plenty of spunk left in the old fellow, and only by grabbing a handful of mane was I able to stay aboard while bringing him back under control.

I pulled him down to a walk, he sighed, went on, and I patted his neck. The feel of leather and the smell of a horse were two things I was always perfectly at home with, but it was never just for fun. From the moment the Nolly Stables arrived in the summer until they left under a blaze of autumn leaves, nothing was on anybody's mind but horse show time — and bringing in as many prizes as possible in Mrs. Nolly's name.

Every move out of place — every stiff hand, every limber ankle — was a matter of greatest scrutiny and practice, for on such small points rested shiny trophies and yards of blue ribbons. On such small points as a smile or lack of it could rest the decision in a class.

Therefore, everything was of optimum importance. It was necessary to keep all the stainless steel, brass, and leather clean; every horse trimmed and brushed as if show day were tomorrow; every feeding precisely measured according to the size and desired weight of the individual animal.

Mrs. Nolly was a real competitor, and that rubbed off on all of us. I would have loads of sore, aching muscles the next morning, but what price glory? For we were beginning another summer, heading into another horse show, and we needed to work harder and better than the year before. Even this joy ride on Major was part of the plan. I had to compete, too, not just help around the stable. But the overriding, ongoing problem for me was not having a horse of my own.

Major and I worked on. My strength was coming back after a winter's "vacation" from riding, and that was a good feeling. When the sun was getting low, I took him up into the rhododendron-infested park above the show grounds. The lane was wide and sandy, and you could hear water trickling out of rocky springs and splashing away to unseen destinations.

The light was so dim that it gave the park a staged look, like in a movie. Lights, action, girl appears on big black Thoroughbred. What silliness. Major nodded as if he guessed my thoughts and agreed, and as I nudged him with my heel, he stepped into a rolling, somewhat hard-to-sit canter, his hooves making soft splatting sounds on the damp ground.

Seeing what appeared to be a limb in the road ahead, I pulled Major up and took a closer look. The limb began wiggling in our direction and I turned Major's head away, hoping he'd neither smelled nor seen it.

The big snake slipped off the road into the thick undergrowth and was gone.

Chapter Three

Mrs. Nolly's stable was a very busy place in the summertime.

While Blowing Rock was a community of only a few hundred citizens in the winter, its cool climate attracted thousands of summer residents. Tourists intrigued with the beautiful Southern Appalachian Mountains kept Rusty's father in business. The old Reinholt Hotel was full to overflowing from the first of June until the first of September, and often later.

So it followed that lots of people wanted to rent horses and take a ride through the beautiful Cone Estate, which was adjacent to the show grounds. That's where Mrs. Nolly came in. She and Carver would take turns driving the battered pink truck up the mountain from Pinehurst, a popular North

Carolina winter resort town, until all thirty-one horses had made the move to their summer quarters.

The shop windows in Blowing Rock sported big posters announcing the Highlands Charity Horse Show. "Be here for the big annual show August the first," they said. "None better in the entire South. Four days of hunters, jumpers, gaited horses, walking horses, cart horses, and ponies. Trophies and ribbons in every class."

Tiny letters at the bottom said, "Your horses will feel fresher and more spirited in the cool, high mountains."

The horse show was the biggest social event of the season, a time of parties and dances, art contests, fireworks displays, and fashion shows. More than five hundred horses would come and, weather allowing, the grandstand was full from early morning until dusk.

I had lived near horses all my life, and now that I was twelve, I couldn't understand what the problem was about buying me one.

"What would we do with it in the wintertime?" That was my mother.

"I don't think we can afford a horse, Chicken." That was my dad.

Not that I didn't win plenty of prizes. The

summer I was eleven, Eva and I tied with four first-place ribbons each. She got two seconds and I won a second and a third. Mrs. Nolly loaned me Major for the hunter classes, or I couldn't have done it. But it still wasn't the same thing as being an owner.

"It's almost the same thing," Mrs. Nolly said. "What would I do if you got a horse and quit working for me? A fine pickle I'd be in."

"You'll have a horse someday," said Carver Coy. "I'd wager it'll be a mighty fine horse."

That night, Mother fried fish, and my Uncle Clus, still smelling like the riverside where he'd sat all day, took the opposite view. "What if you never did get a horse, what then? I never did have a dog. Maybe that's why I spend all my spare time helping out at the animal shelter."

"I don't see what harm just one little old horse would do," I said.

But I felt sorry for Clus, because he cared so deeply about all the stray dogs and puppies that came along, and he spent far too much time and energy tending them at the shelter. There just never seemed to be enough people for all the dogs, and some of them had to be "put to sleep, put out of their misery," he said. He was usually very tired.

There he sat with that thoughtful expression on his smiling, whiskery face.

I persisted. "Dogs and horses aren't the same thing."

"Don't talk back to your Uncle Clus," Mother said above the frying sounds.

"I'm not talking back."

"She is, too," Clus said. "She insists she's got to have a horse."

"What would we do with a horse in the wintertime?" Dad repeated Mom's question. "Cold as it gets here, you couldn't leave it in pasture. And we don't have a barn."

I said, "No problem. Mrs. Nolly could take him to Pinehurst for the winter."

"She's got it all figured out," Mom said to Dad.

"Even decided whether it would be a him or a her," Uncle Clus nodded. He clamped his teeth onto his pipe and sucked at the blue smoke. He looked at me and said, "You sure can be stubborn, Elizabeth."

It was nice to hear my real name for a change, but Dad quickly burst that bubble.

"Oh, the Chicken's got a good head on her shoulders, all right."

I jumped up from the table and said the Famous Four Words that always baffled him so. "Don't call me Chicken!" and I ran from the room, took the stairs three at a time, and piled into my bed.

Chicken sounded nicer when Rusty said it.

"Chicken, could I borrow your snaffle bit to try out on Jack?"

"Sure," I said sweetly.

"Suzanne's still having trouble with him. He pulls all the time. I think that straight-bar bit is too much for his mouth."

"Sure," I said sweetly again.

"You want some help with that saddle? Just give me a minute."

"Sure."

"Can't you say anything but 'sure'?"

"Sure," I said.

He was fourteen, and in the winter he lived in Connecticut, and he had a habit of teasing us Southerners for our accent. But mostly he was nice to everyone, and he went out of his way to be helpful.

Rusty had dark brown eyes like mine and reddish brown hair that stood up in a cow-lick in back. By the time the sun had turned the rest of us pink, Rusty was so brown and his teeth so white by contrast that he could have done a toothpaste commercial.

"Tell you what, Chicken," he said one day.

"Saddle up Tony and I'll put up a triple bar, and we'll see how high he can jump."

"Mrs. Nolly won't like that, Rusty."

"She won't care. Trust me." And I did.

Not that Tony couldn't jump. He was one of the best for teaching beginners how to take small fences, but a triple bar is a big wide jump, and when Tony saw it, he snorted in surprise and refused to go a single step closer.

From the window of her apartment over the tack room, Mrs. Nolly started yelling. From the ring, it sounded like "Whoa!" She came out the door and down the steps as fast as she could, her white hair shining in the afternoon sun.

"Whoa, there!" She panted as she hopped and skipped and got closer. "Rusty Reinholt, what in the dickens are you doing out here on my good horse, Tony? You get down from there."

Rusty got down.

"Jiggs, you know better than this."

"Yes ma'am," I said, flushing.

She caught her breath. "Of all people, Rusty, I would have thought you knew better. Both of you are too old to be galloping faithful old horses up to big fences like this and expecting them to leap right over like two-year-olds."

Rusty handed her Tony's reins as she said, "I'm grounding you, that's what. I don't want you to throw a leg over leather for . . . for a week! The very idea," she scoffed to herself.

By this time, Tony was thoroughly amused at all her shouting and arm-waving. He was practically grinning. Mrs. Nolly put her arms around his neck, burying her face in his fuzzy mane. "Good old boy, nobody's going to treat him badly. Mrs. Nolly promises, yes she does."

Tony stamped his hind legs and swished his tail at a fly.

"I count on you children," Mrs. Nolly said. "And I want your word of honor that this isn't going to happen again, Rusty."

Rusty's high spirits had taken a bad fall. All he could do was nod his head yes.

She was right, of course. Most of the horses in the Nolly Stables were past their prime. They worked hard every day — at least four hours each but seldom more than five — and were hardly colts ready to go jump over the moon. Tony was no more going to jump a fence that size than I was, but the difference was that I knew it. Rusty thought maybe he would. I felt sorry for him now.

No sooner had Mrs. Nolly gotten onto Tony and begun walking him back to the barn that Eva's black limousine came floating down the road behind the grandstand. The horn began to shriek and Tony began to sling his head in spite of Mrs. Nolly's attempts to quiet him. Having had all he could take, he suddenly reared and threw her.

"It was my fault," she grimaced when I helped her up. "No, wait, I'm a little dizzy. I should have known better than to yank back on the reins when he was rearing up. All that noise hurt his ears." That was Mrs. Nolly, ever faithful to her horses.

"I'm terribly, terribly sorry," said the chauffeur, running up to Mrs. Nolly. "I can't drive safely, ma'am, and keep Miss Eva from blowing the horn at the same time."

"It's me, it's me," Eva shouted, oblivious to the accident. "Who wants to go swimming at the country club?"

"Good gravy, Marie," Mrs. Nolly sighed. She was just the shade of a sheet of typing paper when she said, "Elizabeth, find Carver Coy for me. I need him to take me to the hospital. I think my arm is broken."

Chapter Four

She was right. Her right arm was broken in two places just above the wrist, although Mrs. Nolly continued to help around the barn as best she could. Wobbling around on his bowed legs, Carver helped with the feeding and other chores, and Dad started dropping me off earlier in the morning.

For the record, Rusty went swimming at the country club with Eva that day, and I was still pretty ticked off about that.

"Still mad at me, Chicken?"

No comment.

"I waited until Carver took Mrs. Nolly to the doctor."

Still no comment.

"You should have said you needed help with the night feeding. I would have been glad to come back."

I bet.

"Don't look at me that way, Chicken."

But no matter what Rusty said or did — and he was teaching the afternoon classes — I wasn't speaking to him. For one thing, Carver and I were about at our rope's end with all the extra work. Mrs. Nolly drank iced tea, sat on the sun deck outside her apartment, and waved hello down to the customers with her wire coat hanger.

By straightening out a hanger, she could almost reach the itchy places inside the cast on her arm.

It fell to me to exercise Major for her, and these sessions with the black Thoroughbred were the happiest part of my day. I worked him out in the ring while Mrs. Nolly watched approvingly; and I was careful to keep my hands quiet and not start him mouthing and playing with the bit like a colt.

I watched my diagonals carefully, trotting him in a big figure eight and "switching" in the proper places. Starting him from a walk into a canter, I turned his head toward the railing of the ring, nudged him with my heel, and he stepped into the proper lead. The word "lead" refers to the leg with which the horse steps out. To be correct, he should lead with the foreleg closest to the grass, or the inside of the ring.

This gives the horse maximum balance in carrying his rider and is closely watched by judges. It's the reason riders often pull up at horse shows and start their horses off again. It counts against the rider to be unable to get his mount to take the proper lead. However, a horse as experienced as Major would almost second-guess you. He could tell by the shift of your weight which lead he was supposed to take.

"What a beautiful ride," Mrs. Nolly said at the end of a particularly strenuous workout. "I may just let you ride him in the show if this arm of mine keeps acting up the way it is."

I began to daydream about riding Big Boy's Major. He was almost as handsome as William Tell, and I fancied myself beating Eva in all her classes. But I might as well have saved my steam, for within a week, Mrs. Nolly was feeling well enough to ride Major one-handed.

Carver Coy said, "I swear you're going to come right off of there. Maybe even break that other arm." And to me, "She's daffy. Doesn't know what she's doing anymore; her mind's starting to go."

"I am not daffy," Mrs. Nolly said. "I am simply riding my horse. And having a good time. And minding my own danged business!"

"You can't ride a big horse like him one-armed," Carver persisted.

"I can so," said Mrs. Nolly. "You'll see. Major is my good buddy. He won't get me hurt. You must think all I've got is bat brains."

Carver snarled and grumbled and wobbled off down the corridor, giving an occasional pat to the noses reaching out toward him. Things were getting back to normal, and I knew I'd have to forget about showing Major.

The second week in June it rained hard nearly every morning. Classes were called off and Rusty didn't even bother to come by. Customers cancelled and the horses got a long-needed rest, and Carver spent his days checking hooves and resetting shoes.

Saturday was a surprise, though. The weatherman predicted rain, but the sun rose early and began its climb through a sky so blue you would have thought it was October already.

The back meadow was pungent with the smell of the grass. Thistles bloomed in purple and white, and in the woods, trilliums came up pinker than clover. I could hear the wrens and the demands of the gray catbirds; and a nuthatch tapped at the bark of a big oak, looking for bugs.

We turned the horses out and watched them snort and gallop and kick. King, the old bay, snapped at the other horses to frighten them and then settled down to graze.

"We'll never get the dirt off of them if they start rolling," said Carver. And roll they did, scratching their backs on the ground while their legs stuck up in the air.

Mrs. Nolly came out with her dog, Robo, and we all hung over the fence watching.

Horse show time seemed so far away. I dreaded being the girl in the borrowed clothes who rode borrowed horses. King would be a good horse to show in the hunter classes. He was a sandy bay with black trim and he always made a good appearance.

In the hunter competition, judges took everything into consideration, from the rider's habit right down to the conformation — or good looks — of the horse. Thoroughbreds are expected to conform to a standard of beauty, and if ever a horse did, it was Eva's. I was sulking about that when he came galloping past us.

"There never has been a horse like that one," said Mrs. Nolly with a sigh of admiration.

"Aye," said Carver. "He's a dandy." Anything Carver liked, from scrambled eggs to horses, was dandy.

But of course it wouldn't matter so much what horse I rode in equitation, because I would be the one the judge was looking at.

It would be my style of riding and ability to control my horse with little effort that would matter most. I could ride Tony or Jack or Peter and have just as good a chance as the others. I looked at Spots, the dapple gray mare. She took a huge bite of grass and lifted her head. She pricked her ears at something in the distance and then went back to grazing.

The sun was genuinely hot, and I was genuinely tired. The thought of lifting another bale of hay or another bucket of cold spring water made me chill. And there was the cough I'd had lately.

"You've been in too many drafts," Carver said.

"You ought to get that cough seen to," Mrs. Nolly said.

"It's just a cold," I said. But it wasn't.

On June 20th, they took me to the hospital.

Chapter Five

From my window, I could see the limbs of a maple tree brushing against the sky.

Clus made me laugh with his stories of

the old days in Blowing Rock, and he kept the vase on my bed table filled with bright orange daylilies he picked near the animal shelter.

Mrs. Nolly sent brownies, but Carver thought he ought to explain. "I stirred them up. She only put them in the oven," he said.

Eva's mother sent a card saying, "Cheer up, little bird, getting well's the latest word." It showed a woeful-looking owl holding an open umbrella, floating slowly down from a tree. Well, "little bird" was better than little Chicken any day.

Rusty didn't bother to visit, but regularly as clockwork, Dad came by every day on the way home from work.

"How's my little Chicken today? Old Man Pneumonia about caught up with you, little gal."

"Hi, Dad. Do you have to call me Chicken?"

"Does the sun have to come up in the morning?"

"Oh, Dad, come on."

"You get back into bed, girl. You've been told a dozen times to stop hanging out that window. Before you know it, you'll come down really sick. Then bed rest and antibiotics won't be enough to keep you from having to stay here the rest of the summer."

I padded back to bed, got in, and pulled up the covers.

"Perk up your ears and listen, Chicken. I've got something to tell you that I think you are going to like."

Poor Dad. His face was sooty from spending the day working on old plumbing under old houses. His shirt hung out over his belt and his arms were smudged with grease. "I've bought you a horse, Chicken."

I was in a state of shock. My tongue wouldn't do what my brain said for it to do, so finally I just raised up in bed and gave him a big hug. It had sure taken awhile, but he had *done* it.

A small voice came out of me and said, "You've bought me a horse?"

"I hardly bought him for your mom, knowing the way she feels about them and all. Now she'd really be something plunked down on top of a horse, don't you think? But, now, about this fellow.

"The McGimpseys say he doesn't even know it's summer yet. They've had him pastured over in Avery County, and it's a good thousand feet higher up there than it is here. I was up in the high pasture yesterday afternoon and it was as cold as November."

Again I asked, "You've bought me a horse?"

"So," Dad went on, "he's still got most of his winter coat to shed."

"Say you're not putting me on."

"No. I'm not. And he's good-tempered as he can be. Mrs. McGimpsey told me that. They're real nice folks."

"How old?"

"Going on five. They bought him for the grandchildren, but now they want to move back out to Arkansas, and there you are. 'Course, he's good and fat; he needs cleaning up."

Dad started laughing at the expression on my face. "They even say you might get out of here day after tomorrow. I just hope you'll be pleased, honey. And if my favorite girl will be watching that window about ten o'clock in the morning, Carver Coy will bring your new horse around so you can take a look for yourself and see what you think."

I gave Dad another hug. For once he caught me without my mouth full of words.

Suddenly he was gone, and I hadn't asked him a single question.

What color was my horse?

Had he ever been in a show ring?

Could he canter from a standing start or switch leads through a flying figure eight?

Was he gentle or full of tricks?

Would he show spirit or plod about like an old carriage horse?

Could he jump?

I doubted Dad had even bothered to ask any of these things, but inside I had a good feeling, a sense that, as Uncle Clus always said, everything would turn out for the best. For the first time, any prizes I won would be really mine.

I regaled the doctor, the dietician, the orderly, and the nurses with the fact that I was now no longer an exhibitor, I was an owner as well. Mother came to visit after supper. She fluffed up my pillow for me, pulled the spread up to my chin, wished me sweet dreams, and kissed me good night.

And no, she would rather not think about horses, young or old. "What if you fall off one of those big horses?" There was a tinge of worry in her voice and when she left, she gently closed the door behind her. It was her only comment on the matter.

As for me, I settled back to sleep and dream of trophies taller than Rusty Reinholt and so many ribbons that they would have to be stored away in shoe boxes.

My horse would be a deep bay with velvet black trim. People would get him mixed up with King. Or he'd be a bright star-faced sorrel, or maybe a dapper little gray with slate eyes and a soft pinkish nose.

He would be broad-chested and strong from all those years in the high, thin air of the mountains. He would be sure-footed, keen, and clever; he would have all the makings of a winner.

I planned to give him a long, important-sounding show name and he would come out on top of every class we entered. Photographers and reporters would crowd around us and the people would clap and cheer.

In fact, it was about that time that I dreamed I did hear a cheer. And the one voice above them all was Carver Coy's. It was morning. He was outside my window.

He said, "Halloo in there, Miss Elizabeth Mae Jiggsen. You'd better wake up. We came on early; haven't even had breakfast."

I slipped off the edge of the bed and got my slippers on. There was no truck in the drive behind him.

"They wouldn't let Mr. McGimpsey bring his old truck back here. They said it would disturb the patients."

Carver looked down, and when he did I

noticed the rope trailing from his hand. My eyes followed it until I had to lean out the window to see. I should have stayed in bed, for this brought me face to face with my dream horse.

He acknowledged me with a nod, rolled his white eyes back in his head, and gave a mighty sneeze. "A touch of dust, I imagine," said Carver.

He was a bay. And a sorrel. And a kind of dirty beige.

"He's a pinto," I said, not really believing it. "He's just a pony."

Carver came to his defense. "Aye, he does look it, to the casual observer. But he'll measure over the mark, I'm sure of it. And you're just the right size to ride him. Why, put a youngster like yourself up on Beau or Major, and it's like putting a flea on an elephant's back."

Flies swarmed about his eyes and the pinto shook his head at them. They flew away, hovered, then lit again in a black pulsing colony across his face. To make matters worse, his forelock, mane, and tail were a mass of last autumn's cockleburs.

"It makes a better show to have a horse and rider matched for size," Carver reasoned, letting me down easy. "I know what I'm

34

talking about. Of course, his coat needs work."

I moaned to myself, just short of crying. A coarse blanket of winter hair was bunched in muddy clumps all over him. The hair around his fetlocks was long and curly and thick with sticktights. His hooves were big and uneven.

"I've not seen many feet in worse shape than these," Carver said. "We'll just have to work on him and see what can be done."

"I don't want him," I said. "I won't have him."

"Well, you've got him, and you ought to be grateful for your father's good intentions, too. We'll just have to do the best we can with what we've got to work with, now won't we? And the very first thing Dr. Coy prescribes is a rigid diet. If he gets much heavier, we'll have a full-blown case of founder on our hands."

I said, "He has glass eyes," referring to his whitish pupils.

"They aren't bothering him, why should they be bothering you?"

Once again he rolled his eyes, triggering another sneeze.

"He's even got a cold."

"I rather think he's been grazing chest

deep in an early crop of goldenrod. Something's just tickling his nose."

"I don't care," I said to Carver. "*This* is my dream horse? I'd have to get better to die — of embarrassment."

"Be miserable, Elizabeth. Just go on and be as miserable as you want to. Me, I've got work to do."

As Carver led him away, I wailed, "But it's a pinto."

He plodded along on his broken hooves. I could hear him scampering up the ramp into Mr. McGimpsey's truck. Then I heard the sounds of the big engine. It groaned and pulled away.

I half-heartedly thanked Dad that night, and Mother let me have it after he left.

"You ought to be ashamed of yourself! Your father has worked hard to earn the money for your horse, and all you can bring yourself to do is stare at the walls. He was so hurt. I'd be ashamed, Elizabeth."

I was. I kept thinking what the other kids would say, and it wasn't long before I found out for myself, because it seems like anything you dread to have happen, happens right away. Before I could turn around twice, a dreamless night had passed, the nurse helped me into my things, Dad signed the release papers, and we were on our way to Mrs. Nolly's.

Dad's rickety panel truck rattled up to the front of the stable, and I climbed out.

"Good-bye, Chicken."

"Bye-bye, Dad."

As if on cue, Eva's chauffeur pulled in right behind the truck and out stepped Eva with a bouncing of straw curls and a rustle of clean, starched clothes. She dismissed her driver with a wave.

"What's this I hear about you having a new horse, Chicken? Is he anything like William Tell?"

Chapter Six

"I don't know what it is, but whatever it is, it certainly isn't like Garry," Eva said. She used William Tell's nickname.

"It's a pinto," I said.

"It looks like a circus pony," Eva said back.

"It does not."

"Manners, ladies," Mrs. Nolly reminded us.

"Well, I don't care. It's a perfectly awful-looking beast. I wouldn't put my good saddle on it, I know that much."

The perfectly awful-looking beast nipped Eva's arm and drew a short high shriek of pain from her.

"Be watchful of that soft mouth," Carver said from his bent-over position next to the pinto. "I suspect he has sharp teeth after a whole night of so little to eat."

"Well, I'm not going to say any good things about him, ever. And I'm not staying here another second!"

Eva rubbed the bitten arm and stalked off into the corridor where her words grew steadily lower. "That mean, old, perfectly stupid, and horrible pinto beast!"

The pinto nickered and rolled his eyes. This brought on a sneeze, as usual. He pulled his foreleg and Carver let him have it back. Carver got up wearily and said, "I was about to let him cramp up. Giving him a rest is a good idea, because I don't think he's used to having his feet handled much. He'd be easy spoiled. Whoa there, Little Jack Horner, my man. You can stop blowing your horn. The mean old man is resting himself awhile."

The pinto nipped and squealed and shook his head belligerently.

Through all of this, Mrs. Nolly sat comfortably on a hay bale.

"Let me tell you what I see, Elizabeth," she said.

"I can't see anything in him," I said, but she went right on.

"For one thing, he has a fine sense of humor." Mrs. Nolly narrowed her eyes at my dream horse. "You can see it around his mouth and eyes. Some have it and some just don't. I have seen many a bitter horse going about with his ears laid flat to his neck and a kind of bored, menacing expression."

It made me think of Spots, and I said her name without thinking.

"Yes, Spots is a little that way," Mrs. Nolly agreed.

That gave Carver an opportunity to get in on the conversation.

"Aye, and she's not much of a worker, Spots. In half an hour, she's ready to come home. That's not this fellow's style. You should have seen Mrs. Petersen trying to manage Spots and stay in the saddle at the same time. Day before yesterday, wasn't it?"

"She wasn't gone fifteen minutes when Spots just turned around and started back home. And being something of a timid rider,

Mrs. Petersen just didn't want to pull too hard on her mouth," Mrs. Nolly said.

"Which Spots figured out," Carver put in, "there being nothing wrong with her brain."

"We heard her long before we saw her, don't you know, yelling, 'Whoa, sweet horsy; whoa, little sweetness.' Spots brought her right on home, of course. Waited for her to climb down and went directly inside to her stall. It didn't do a whole lot for the reputation of the barn, I imagine. I promised Mrs. Petersen a free ride on Stogy to make up for it."

"Get back to what you were saying," said Carver.

"Well, sometimes you'll find a patient kind of horse, who'll put up with most anything, and usually has to. He just does his work well and lets it go at that. He's sort of a private person, you understand, and he's not making any permanent arrangement about whom he likes to have ride him. He has no tricks, but then he won't be remembered for any great spirit."

"Then there's the sleepy heads and the vicious ones no one ever treated right from the beginning," Carver said.

"But this one has a laugh or two hiding behind those glassy eyes," said Mrs. Nolly.

"And the awful thing," I said, "is that the laugh's on me."

"I suppose you expected Man O' War to come stepping off Mr. McGimpsey's old truck," Carver said.

"We've all had that kind of dream, Carver."

He said, "And here I thought we had her jollied up."

"Admit it, Mrs. Nolly," said Mrs. Nolly teasingly, talking to herself. "When you first saw this little fellow, you had your doubts. But in the morning light, and after getting a little better acquainted . . ."

She began to walk around him, running a critical eye over his legs and chest and pudgy barrel.

Knowing he was the subject of their conversation, the pinto basked in the glow of the old woman's smile. He arched his neck a little and blinked his eyes proudly.

"Look at him!" Carver laughed, slapping his hands.

"He may be smiling," I admitted, "but he still looks awful."

Mrs. Nolly was talking to herself again. "You know, Mrs. Nolly, at first you thought you'd work all summer and not be able to make anything out of him. But you were dead wrong, old girl." She was trying to persuade herself and me, it seemed.

That annoyed Carver, who carried most of the work load these days. "*Who* is it that's going to work all summer? You just tend to your busted arm and let us fellows do the work."

Us fellows, I thought. It was true. I was one of the guys, all right.

"Now, you sit back down on your bale of hay, please ma'am, and let one of the hired hands explain it all to you," Carver went on.

The pinto, seeming to sense my unhappiness, ignored me.

"So," Carver began. "It will take about a week to get that extra hundred pounds off him. And in that time, he'll have all the water he can drink, but very little else. Except for a chunk of hay and a small measure of oats twice a day, and a touch of bran to take the starch out of him. Don't you say one single word," he said to us.

Mrs. Nolly closed her mouth. So did I.

"Monday will be the first of July and that's the day he's to have his bath. Until then, I don't want anyone putting more than a damp sponge to him, and that only to his face. I hope to get rid of all these flies, is all. But stuck in here without any exercise, and without even the sunshine of a meadow, he might catch a dose of sniffles.

"His hooves are sound and solid, and I plan to have them in show shape in another week or two."

I thought, to what end? What could a pinto possibly be shown in at a show the size of Highlands?

"Don't ask that question," said Carver Coy, as I opened my mouth. "Okay, diet and hooves. That's done. Bath on the first day of July. And between now and then, someone's got work to do on this mane and tail. Never have I seen such a mess in my life."

"I'm elected," I said mournfully.

"That's the most you'll get to do until he's ready for riding," said Mrs. Nolly. "I've talked on the phone with your mother, and I've made her a promise that we won't let you get yourself exhausted again."

"Then we'll see what we've got," Carver said, "and not until then."

"What could he possibly be shown in?"

"That was the question I just told you not to ask," Carver said. "Give me some time, girl. I'm a horseman, not a magician."

"Rather fun," sighed Mrs. Nolly. "Who

can tell? We might even wind up with a silk purse."

Carver grimaced. "Or a sow's ear," he said. "Aye, it could go either way."

Chapter Seven

Everything seemed to run together.

Eva started doing her own saddling and rode out in the mornings without a word to any of us. Garrison's Quarter, alias William Tell, took those long, ground-skimming strides more beautifully than any horse I'd ever seen in my life. But it was a horse of an entirely different color and disposition who stood grudgingly still on July the first, taking the first bath of his life.

Carver slopped sudsy water over his back, rubbing the dirty hair with a sponge. The pinto, now called Mr. Ragman (one of Mrs. Nolly's split-second inspirations), quietly nipped at the old man's back pockets while Carver cried. "Who's watching this horse's fiddle head, now!"

Outside, it was a songbird's day, but here

in the barn, the light played dimly between the slats of the stalls.

Carver said, "Bring me that bucket, there, Elizabeth. Don't strain yourself."

Rusty, who was helping Carver, said, "He means you, Chicken."

I'd barely taken two steps when I spilled the bucket down the front of my jeans.

"You know where the hose is," Carver said.

I bent over to pick up the bucket, and the pinto nudged me with his nose. Down I went, smack on my face in the dirt corridor.

"You know where the soap is," Mrs. Nolly said from her seat on a nearby bale.

"The Chicken's just addled over her beautiful horse," Rusty teased.

"Hush," Mrs. Nolly ordered him, and he promptly shut up.

The pinto's coat came out lustrous and clean, but there was still his mane and tail, an impossible-seeming task. When Carver and Mrs. Nolly went off to attend to other matters, I got down to work on his matted tail.

"You aren't going to get anywhere at that rate," Rusty said.

"You shut your face," I said.

"Look, start at the bottom of the tail and

work up." As Rusty worked on, bits of the matted burrs began to fall away from the tangled hair. He gave me a long look, a kind of see-there look.

"Where's that all-American, kind-to-animals girl who won the junior sportsmanship trophy a couple of years ago?"

"I don't care what anybody says," I told him. "I don't have to like this horse, and nobody can make me."

The pinto stamped angrily at an imaginary fly.

"Well, you may not care, Miss Smart Pants, but he cares. And so do I. And if you don't want him, give him to me. I've never owned a horse and I'm certainly not prejudice against pintos."

"You'll get to ride Beau. You won't have to worry how you'll look. But me, I wind up with this, this —"

"For your information, Chicken — as if you're even interested — it's just four more weeks 'till show time. Out of five or six hundred horses, you can bet not too many of them are going to leave here as winners. Even Eva's big horse is going to have stiff competition. There'll be people here who have been showing for twenty-five years and more. They know all the tricks of the trade, and then some."

"So?"

"So, anybody who fills out an entry blank had better be prepared to be a good loser, just in case."

I don't know what made me do it, but right then I picked up a bucket of spring water and dumped it over his head. He blubbered and sputtered, the bucket looking like a tin tophat on him.

Rusty went back to work, and this time he wasn't speaking.

The first time up on Mr. Ragman was unreal. He didn't pay a whole lot of attention to my tugs on the reins, but seemed to turn easily to the pressure of my heels. A touch behind the girth on the right side would make him back around and turn right. I couldn't figure it out.

I sat on a fence rail, holding his reins and feeling sorry for myself.

Toby whizzed around the ring on Stogy, posting way too high and holding his hands out at a funny angle in front of him. Mrs. Nolly dozed on her sun deck and Carver's anvil rang with the hammering. The July sun beat down so hard that the ordinarily dappled shade of the trees became a deep, cool black.

I kept thinking, why can't somebody else

be wrong for once? Why can't they see this "Mr. Ragman," horse of many colors, for what he is: A pinto barely bigger than a pony and completely out of it when it came to conformation judging. Mrs. Nolly's dog Robo looked better to me right then. And I still felt tired. And Eva. All she ever did was call him "a mean, old, perfectly stupid, awful horrible pinto beast." That was rubbing it in with salt.

She was still mad at him for biting her, and that was the one thing that made me feel a certain kinship with my little horse. It was as if both of us were underdogs having to fight our way up in the world together. But the Highlands Horse Show? Forget it.

The show grounds soon would be crowded with horses from Connecticut and Texas, Kentucky and Florida. There would be walkers and standard breds, Thoroughbred hunters and jumpers, Morgans and harness horses with papers as long as the mountain winter.

And in the midst of all this would be Elizabeth Jiggsen, riding in clothes loaned to her by Suzanne. It was such a thoroughly frustrating thought that I tried not to dwell on it, but did anyway. It was like somebody saying, "Don't think about elephants." That's all that comes to mind.

There was simply no comparing this raggedy little pinto to the horseflesh he'd be competing against. So far, I didn't even know if he could jump over a mud puddle.

That night, Uncle Clus came to dinner. Just in from another fishing trip, he was wearing his green wading boots and a khaki helmet and jungle suit which he once said were left over from so long ago, he'd just rather not talk about it.

There was a heavy smell about him and enough fish for us all. "Nearest nothing I about ever saw," he told Mother, "but maybe you can do something with them."

The sun glinted in his eyes when he turned to look at me. "You look a whole lot better standing up than lying down in a hospital bed."

"She's got roses in her cheeks," Dad said, "she sure does."

Clus scratched the white froth of his beard. "Let's you and me mosey out to the veranda and have a little chat."

Mother said, "I wish somebody would talk this child out of riding those big horses. It simply scares me to death. She was up on that Major horse of Mrs. Nolly's. I saw her myself when I drove past the show ground today."

"Ah," said Uncle Clus, "she sticks to a

saddle like a fly to flypaper. I doubt she'll ever fall, Marie."

"The horse could fall down; it just worries me to death."

"I know, I know," Clus said. "But you rest easy. It's folks like you and me who can't even go down stair steps without getting dizzy. But the girl's all right."

The girl frankly didn't think so, but I followed Clus out the front door and took a seat in one of the lawn chairs. He eased himself down on a rocker, his stiff knee bothering him. He laid the crutch where he could get it with his right hand.

"Elizabeth, I want you to tell your father how grateful you are for your new horse."

"I did thank him," I said defensively.

"Oh, I don't mean just with words. I mean for you to say it and mean it."

"Yes, sir."

"You're just being as cantankerous as the very devil."

"Yes, sir," but I really didn't think so.

"Now I know your horse isn't much compared to those tall, silky ones. But compared to nothing, he's a whole heck of a lot."

I said, "I was doing okay with nothing. And I could have ridden Spots."

Clus pulled on his pipe and let his eyes drift away from me.

"You see yourself in a certain way, my dear," the old man said another puff later. "You see yourself being like Eva — having everything Eva has. And because you don't, you're mad at the world."

"I am not."

"Be quiet," he said. "You are too. Now. I was once your age, you know, and it wasn't much fun for me, either. All because there was a boy named Dicky Dodds, the only boy in the territory with a big white mule that could drink soda pop out of a bottle. He was partial to Brown Cow, I think it was called. Anyhow, it was some kind of chocolate drink."

I stared off into the Johns River Gorge, watching clouds rise toward the pink sunset.

"Oh, I thought I hated old Dicky, of course. I had a long list of reasons for feeling that way. But all the time I was just hating myself because I wasn't Dicky Dodds instead of Clus Jiggsen and because I didn't have a mule like Daisy and a quarter for every time some summer resident wanted to see her throw back her head and guzzle a pop."

"I'd rather have a mule over that pinto," I said.

"Don't be curt with your old uncle who means well. Because you, my dear, have nothing to be sorry about. You're like a little butterfly that goes sailing out one morning and finds no flowers. You're still a butterfly; you still have wings. You can go right up the sky, if you want to, and on your own power."

Some butterfly, I thought.

"You're just sorry you aren't Dicky Dodds. It matters not about the name — Eva, Dicky — it's all the same bucket of clams. It all comes down to what you feel inside. You should be a little kinder to yourself, Elizabeth. After that, it comes easy being kind to others. And that includes muddy pintos covered up with burrs, too."

"I didn't come out here to be lectured," I said.

"Hush that talk, now. I wouldn't bother to lecture you, would I, if I didn't care about you?"

"I'll thank Dad. It's not his fault. He doesn't know about horses."

Clus said, "That may be. But when that horse of yours grins at you, I'd advise you to grin back. It won't cost anything. It might do you some good."

He was finished. He relaxed his weight in

the rocker and gazed out upon the deep, lush forests. The breeze came up and stirred the trees. The rain finally drove us inside, washing the air clean of butterflies and skillet smoke.

Chapter Eight

It was a terrible daydream.

The horse show was in full swing. Eva was riding William Tell, and right beside her was Rusty, riding Beau. There were more than thirty other riders, all beautifully mounted and attired when suddenly the ringmaster called for a walk. One more entry was to be admitted to the ring.

The end gate opened wide and in I rode on the pinto. At first I heard some polite giggling, but it soon developed into outright laughter. "Isn't she sweet?" someone said. "Bringing her little pony into the ring with all the big horses."

It was the worst dream of my life, and it was a relief when it faded away and I realized Saturday morning was still in progress

— with me in it, lifesize and real. The grand-stand was as empty as the box seats. Not a soul was in sight except for Mrs. Nolly. Holding her injured arm protectively to her side, she reined Major onto the grassy center of the ring and backed him carefully.

Then she turned him and urged him into a sudden, furious gallop that brought him by leaps and bounds to the gate where I was waiting.

"I told you so!" Mrs. Nolly trumpeted. "I told you I was just as good with my left hand. Good fellow, good old boy. How about a carrot, now."

On cue, I pulled one from my back pocket and held it out to the rangy gelding.

"You're going to bust more than that good right arm," Carver yelled from the breeze-way of the big barn.

"Listen to that," Mrs. Nolly whispered. "You'd think he owned me or something."

Finally I went to the barn. Carver was finishing up on Mr. Ragman and I thought I ought to take a look. I had to admit I was surprised.

The little horse stood proudly, four-square and straight, no trace left of the burrs and muddy clumps. Gone, too, was the fuzzy mane that had made him look like the chubby, chatty pony from the book *Black Beauty*.

He was almost handsome.

"I roached back his mane," Carver explained. "It made his neck seem too heavy to suit my taste. And if you ask me, it's an overwhelming improvement over what he was to begin with. Slimmed down like he is, this little fellow has a nice shape. He's easy on the eyes, is what he is."

The pinto was doing its "Hey, look me over" routine, its bluish eyes glistening.

Carver went on. "Now, about his hooves. They're in much better shape than I had expected. I don't think the founder got to them, or if it did, there's no sign of damage now. See that he gets some vitamins along with his feed, Elizabeth. It'll be the source of his stamina for the hard training he needs."

I said to myself, "Training for what, a pony cart?"

Carver picked up on that immediately. I guess I deserved it when he said, "And don't you be looking at me like I'd done you an injustice when I've been up since daylight finishing work on this little dickens. You might say just one little thank you," he huffed.

"I'm sorry, Carver. I'll try to do better."

"And you could be a little nicer to young Mr. Reinholt in the future. He's done his share of the work in your interest."

"Oh, is that right?"

"Yes, he has," Carver rambled on. "Plus which, just let me leave you with this thought: 'For want of a nail, the shoe was lost; for want of a shoe, the horse was lost; and for want of a horse, the rider was lost.' Ben Franklin put that little ditty together. You keep it in mind, now.

"Give him another try, child. Don't give up on him so soon."

I mounted Mr. Ragman. He reined neither left nor right: it was the same old story. And he was used to such a collected little trot that he must have looked like a sleepy pony moving along in the sun-dappled shade.

Urged on, he would break into an equally collected canter — a feeling far different from what I experienced on Mrs. Nolly's lanky, long-legged hunters. And he seemed to turn by accident rather than on command. He would stop dead in his tracks at the slightest touch to the reins, then back up immediately unless the pressure in his mouth was relieved.

After an hour of this, I was fairly certain

there was no hope for him. I already knew I wouldn't have a chance at the Highlands Horse Show, and I headed him home.

"Let Rusty give him a try," Mrs. Nolly said.

I said, "No."

"Come on, Chicken, I won't hurt your pony. Honestly."

Carver said, "He's not a pony. I have to keep telling everyone."

Rusty bounded up into the saddle, patted the pinto's neck, teased his ears, and laughed at him. The pinto seemed to enjoy all this immensely.

Rusty worked him in small circles in the breezeway, announcing to my surprise, "For one thing, he's trained to neck-rein."

"You'll catch onto it, dear," said Mrs. Nolly. "He'll be handy in the equitation classes."

"Nobody can beat you, if you concentrate on equitation," Carver said. "It won't matter what horse you ride, just how you ride."

They had it all figured out, didn't they?

"For another thing," Rusty said, "this little man of yours will turn in the direction in which you lean your weight." He demonstrated and I watched as the pinto moved first to one side, then to the other.

Carver couldn't stop hooting about it. "I'll be, what do you think? He's not untrained, he's overtrained, that's what."

Mrs. Nolly went into giggling spasms. "I've never seen a horse go through his paces with such little effort in my life, so help me."

Rusty took the pinto into a tight right-hand circle at a trot. When he came back to the starting point, he broke into a canter on the left lead and made another equally tight left-hand circle. It was a perfect figure eight.

I swallowed and looked again as Rusty took him back through the maneuver. It was incredible. Rusty stopped him, backed him, and put him back in place — all with unseen signals.

Then he dropped the reins on the pinto's neck and said, "If you don't want him, really and truly, I'd like to borrow him for the equitation classes."

"He's a winner," Mrs. Nolly said. "And after all the things you said."

But he's the color of the rainbow, I grumbled to myself. And he's small and compact whereas the other equitation horses would be lean and long. I recalled my bad dream, and it left me with an empty feeling.

"I'll tell you your problem," Carver said.

"You've never ridden a western horse. That's how he's been trained."

I gazed at the pinto and he gazed back at me. He seemed to be saying, "There, big shot. How do you like my style?"

Rusty kept teasing his ears until the horse shook his head violently and stamped his feet.

"He's as clean as a pin," Mrs. Nolly said, "as pretty as a picture." But what kept going through my mind was that Mr. Ragman struck them as cute and versatile. He was like a mascot for the Nolly Stables.

That's when Carver said, "We oughta make him our mascot, Mrs. Nolly."

Rusty was a bit too long-legged for him, but he repeated what he had said. "Really. I could ride him in equitation and it'd be no contest. I think he would practically obey voice commands."

"Okay," I said, as I saddled up. "Let's get it over with."

The minute a new horse arrives at the Nolly Stables, everyone starts speculating whether he can jump or not.

A horse that "hunts" doesn't have to take the big jumps. His form is what counts, and for this reason, a hunter is usually a Thoroughbred. That means he has strength and stamina and good looks. Although some Thoroughbreds tend to be skinny and frail like Stogy, the stockier horses look better in the field.

A jumper, on the other hand, must be able to clear the big fences. These are set up inside the ring and will "knock down," or come apart, in the event a horse or rider falls on one. A jumper has to have strength and stamina just like a hunter, but he doesn't have to have pure bloodlines. He simply has to be a horse, even a pinto. Even a small pinto.

Even Mr. Ragman.

Because some of the fences are five feet and higher, jumping can be very dangerous. To quote my mother: "Oh, dear Lord, you're not going to get up on those big horses and go over those big fences, are you?" And that's the way most mothers — and dads — feel about it.

At horse shows, jumping provides the biggest thrills, and spills. The crowds literally leap to their feet as the excitement builds and the competition starts getting keen. I'd won sixth place one time on Tony, but now that Tony was getting a few years on him, Mrs. Nolly had decided his jumping days were over. Naturally, I'd concentrated on hunters since that. But this was something else. Here I was, sitting on this blocky little horse, staring down the center of the ring at the jump Rusty had put up. We started toward it at a trot.

Much to my surprise, the pinto popped right over it, broke into a spirited canter on the other side, and obeyed my signals just as he had Rusty's. It was hard getting used to it, but with a little circling, and a little leaning this way and that, I was beginning to like this strange way of doing things. The pinto hardly took a deep breath.

"Do it again," Carver yelled. "Be ready for him to balk on you."

Off we went, and it happened all over again. From an easy-going canter, he gathered himself and sprang gracefully over a single bar resting on its pegs three feet off the ground.

Rusty set the jump six inches higher; Mr. Ragman sailed right over it.

Carver was clapping and whistling, while Mrs. Nolly made do by slapping her good hand against a board.

Up to the fence I cantered him, brought him to a sliding stop, and backed him three steps. He was as handy as a quarter horse, but Rusty was right. I didn't know there were horses with push buttons on them, and it was taking some getting used to.

"He can jump," said the incredulous Mrs. Nolly. "Some kid has been riding him over creeks and logs all his young life, I bet."

Carver slapped his hand along the pinto's neck and said, "He can go right over the moon if he's a mind to."

They were right about one thing. He would be an excellent horse for equitation classes. While other children were tugging at the reins, I would be guiding my horse along with the unseen pressure of a knee or heel. My hands would remain motionless, and that would count greatly in my favor.

Rusty put the fence up another notch, but the pinto shied on the approach, and we concluded that he needed a good deal of polishing, talented though he was. The thing now was to be sure he didn't get hurt in training, not to tire him out or bore him by showing him the same old jumps over and over. It was essential that he continue to like jumping.

The cogs and wheels in Elizabeth Jiggsen's brain began to work. I could ride him in equitation this year, but keep training him as an open jumper. By next year, he might be good enough to attract a buyer. I would ask enough money to buy a hunter, a better one than Eva's — if such a horse existed.

The pinto grinned at me, but no matter what I'd promised Uncle Clus, I just couldn't grin back. I was plotting to get rid of Mr. Ragman and buy the horse of my dreams. After all, I thought, who wouldn't.

No matter how much hard work lay ahead, it would be well worth it.

Chapter Nine

Carver's enthusiasm over Mr. Ragman almost equaled his enthusiasm over Benny, his gentle old walking horse.

He'd gaze off into the sky and say, "You don't even have to pace him. He knows exactly when to take off. I think he could go high, with more work. I tell you, Elizabeth, there's something about that little guy. He's a standout. You keep schooling him for equitation, but set those jump pegs on up there.

"Watch he doesn't get bored, now. Yes, he's got style, and he's got a catchy name.

He'll be a crowd favorite, all right. Aim for the top."

I took his advice, careful not to reveal to anyone my secret plan. After another week's work, Mr. Ragman was jumping the four-foot rail without any qualms. On days when there was lots of saddling and bridling to be done for the customers, Rusty worked him out for me. After just two weeks, the pinto was up to four and a half feet, and eager to go higher.

It didn't seem to matter to him what he jumped. It could be a chicken coop out on the hunt field, a sheet held between Mrs. Nolly and Carver Coy, or one of the jumps in the ring. He danced about like a colt and was getting to be something of an item with our regular riders. Some of them started staying late in the afternoons to watch him work.

We were a couple of weeks away from the horse show when it occurred to me I might possibly enter him in jumping instead of equitation. Maybe I could sell him a year earlier than planned. Maybe I was closer to my dream horse than I'd thought.

Everybody worked harder. Rusty rode Beau early every morning and the kids started coming for two classes a day. Everyone was polishing his riding skills, for we all wanted Mrs. Nolly to be proud of us. Eva kept her distance from Mr. Ragman and me, and Mrs. Nolly tried to make the point that life can be difficult for rich children. They never know whether their friends are real friends or just freeloaders looking for invitations to fancy parties. "Eva could be jealous of you," Mrs. Nolly said. That was about the most ridiculous thing I'd ever heard. Why would she be jealous of me? Guessing my question, Mrs. Nolly answered it: "Making friends is easy for you; no strings are attached. Eva wishes she could trust people, too." If so, she had a weird way of showing it.

Once Eva'd started calling me "Jiggsie," it got to be habit. She said Mr. Ragman was vicious. And one day she said, "I hope you fall on your face, Jiggsie Jiggsen." That did it.

I was soaping down Eva's muddy saddle girth, and when I looked up at all that curly blonde hair, I knew there was only one thing to do. I dumped the pan of water over her head.

Rusty got mad all over again. "You think the entire world revolves around you," he told me that day. "Well, it doesn't. Eva may not be the friendliest person in town, but that's no reason for you to go off half-cocked, dumping filthy water on her. She can't help the way she is; she's always been that way. But you should know better."

His face was scarlet.

That night, so was Mother's.

But instead of being angry, Mrs. McCormack only called Mother to ask her to try to get me to be more understanding of Eva's "growing pains."

Well, girls will be girls, I supposed.

Mother had a different interpretation of what had happened.

"Now, Elizabeth, you know how temperamental Eva can be, but I expect you to behave sensibly at all times and under all circumstances. Use your head. I want you to keep this whole matter in perspective."

"Why doesn't *she* have to be the level-headed one?"

"Don't talk back to your mother," mother said.

"Everybody takes up for Eva!" I started to cry.

"I'm sure she's hurt your feelings," Dad added. "She may have said some very cutting things."

And Mother said, "But that's no reason

for you to develop the same bad habits. You're my little girl, and I expect you to mind your manners. The McCormacks will have to deal with Eva. But we love you, and you're the one we're concerned about."

Right that minute, it didn't seem that way. It seemed that everybody understood Eva, but nobody understood Elizabeth.

As the days got busier, I confined my workouts to early morning like Rusty did. Eva had become a midday rider, and while she concentrated on the task of winning every class on her schedule, her dueling with me came to a stop. We ignored each other. In her mind, I guess, I was beaten before I even started.

Eva's willowy red bay was shaping up beautifully. I was certain he would win the conformation hunter class; and no one denied that Eva was a fine horsewoman. She was pouring so much work into her riding, she would probably deserve to win. However, that made me only feel more like a dowdy duck trying to become a svelte swan.

Carver did all he could to bolster my spirits and I helped him groom Benny morning and night. The old horse was still quite beautiful, and when he moved, his high-stepping grace was all his own.

Much to the dismay of many walking horse owners, some trainers used cruel means to make their horses perform. They put acid on the sensitive skin above the horses' front heels, and this made the horses reach for the sky with their stinging front legs. At the same time, they squatted down in back in an effort to take the weight off their front hooves.

"Some people think that looks good," Carver said, "but to me it's the awfulest thing that ever was. And people like Garson Gambill even give them stimulants and tranquilizers and then go into the show ring and beat the rest of us.

"Well, this year, we'll just see who wins."

It was the same thing Carver Coy said every summer, and every summer Garson Gambill won practically all the trophies.

Carver took a deep breath. "I'll beat the stuffings out of him this time," he said. "I'll get out my old brown suit with the red satin lining in the coat. When the sun hits that lining, Elizabeth, that judge won't be able to see anything else.

"If only something could be proved against him. His horses are fine-blooded, I'll hand him that. But no creature deserves that kind of treatment."

"We could post a complaint with the horse show manager," I said.

"Sure, but who's to put up the fifty dollar fee? I don't have that much money."

Clus had come to visit at the stable that day. He had been thoughtful and quiet, but now he took the old pipe from his mouth and said, "Well, we'll raise the money somehow. Things will always work out for the best."

"Hello up there," someone called from below.

None other than Garson Gambill himself. He called up again to the sun deck where we were sitting watching the vans arrive. An enormous roan stallion moved uneasily under him.

"Not talking, are you? We'll see about that when the Gambill Stables take home all the prizes. Right, Mr. Coy?"

"I'm not speaking to you," Carver told him, "because you're no friend of mine — or anybody who loves a walking horse for its pure and unadulterated beauty. That's why I'm not talking to you."

"Then wait and see," said Garson Gambill with the shade of his derby's brim slanting down his face. "I'll make a believer out of you."

"Well, before you do that, you better move out of the way of that snake right beside you."

Gambill took the roan up so sharply in the mouth that it bolted sideways. Gambill was nearly dumped off, and I was laughing so hard I barely heard his snarled farewell. "I don't think that was in the least bit funny, Mr. Coy, and I'll show you how unfunny I think it really was one of these days. You, too, Princess Giggles."

Gambill swung the horse back around. He wasn't gone yet.

"I know what you people think of me," he said. "Don't think I haven't got ears. You think I give drugs to my horses to make them perform right. You never stop to think that I might just be a superior horseman capable of keeping even the most difficult animal under control at all times."

"Hogwash," said Carver. "You near-about got thrown right then."

"That's the way you feel, is it? Well, where do you suppose I'd be today if I hadn't become the superior horseman I am? I'd be back home in Fayetteville, hanging wallpaper and installing carpets with my Daddy and brother. And I'm an outdoor type, always have been. Walking around on my knees all day — pasting up wallpaper — it kills my soul."

Carver said firmly, "You're doing something to those horses, and I know it for a fact," and for the moment, Gambill gave up. He rode away.

Mrs. Nolly was half asleep in the warm sun. Without opening her eyes, she said, "That was probably the wrong thing to do, Carver, but I bet it felt good to get one on him."

We basked in the sunshine, taking a well-deserved rest.

"Well, things will always work out," Clus concluded.

No sooner were the words out of his mouth than Gambill rode back to the sun deck.

"You lazy people up there! Who's responsible for all these dogs?"

"Why, I am," said Uncle Clus. He got up shakily and leaned over the sun deck railing. "How do you do, I'm Clus Jiggsen, and those little dogs are with me."

"Counting the puppies, there's twenty-four dogs down here. What are you trying to do, start an animal shelter?"

Clus said, "To tell you the truth, I'm trying to put one out of business."

Gambill said, "As soon as the show secretary gets here, I'll have these mongrels drummed right off the show grounds — and you with them."

"Shame on you, Mr. Gambill," Clus said. "My dogs need homes. When people don't come to the shelter, why sometimes I take the shelter to them. At the May Day celebration over at the school, I found homes for sixteen little dogs. I thought the horse show would be an excellent place — "

"Why don't you take these flea-eaten beasts and scram! They scare my horses! And teasing me about a snake that wasn't even there could have got me thrown!"

"A good horseman is safe under all conditions," Mrs. Nolly boomed, "as long as the horse stays afoot, of course."

Gambill's eyes darkened, narrowed, squinted, and then shifted back and forth across us. He glared and glowered, and then snapped his crop in the air as though to hit Clus's motley, happy dogs. Then he left.

"I don't know exactly how to describe that man," Carver mused as Gambill and his horse grew smaller in the distance.

"I'd say he snapped at us," Mrs. Nolly said. "Or maybe 'snarl' is a better word for it."

I got up, stretched, and took a look at all the commotion taking place around us.

Horses were everywhere on the show grounds. The temporary stalls with their bright striped awnings covered the hillside across from the hunt field. Here and there, bunches of yellow daisies stood in clumps, reaching for the sun.

It wouldn't be long now.

Chapter Ten

With only four more days to show time, Eva lamed her big beautiful horse. She rode him once too often in Rock Creek and bruised the sole of his left hind hoof.

"What a terrible thing to have happen," said Mrs. Nolly. "I don't guess he'll be sound enough to show, Eva. I'm sorry, dear."

For lack of anyone to blame, Eva turned to me and yelled, "It's all your fault!" She called her chauffeur and went home without another word.

"Don't pay any attention," Mrs. Nolly said. "Just tend to your own business and let Eva attend to hers."

I decided to do that, for once. The horses were taking my full attention now that so little time remained. Hair had to be shaved from ears and muzzles, from fetlocks and from around the coronet band of the hooves. Carver reset shoes until he was blue in the face and I brushed horses until they glistened.

I put Toby to work cleaning snaffle bits and stirrups. Suzanne pitched in, and the little Bledsoe twins offered to help Mrs. Nolly put out the feed to give me more time to school Mr. Ragman.

"I can do that for you," Rusty said. "Remember, I believed in him before you did."

"No, thank you."

"You don't have to be so huffy."

"I said no, thank you."

"Come on, Chicken. Why are you mad at me? Maybe you do have a right to be mad at Eva."

"I am certainly not mad at Eva," I said. "I haven't got the vaguest idea what you're talking about."

I rode Mr. Ragman in the park for about a half hour. He seemed fairly relaxed, whereas I felt tense. Mrs. Nolly had begun to talk about putting us in the jumper competition, and while I was uncertain about it, I thought it might be worth the try.

The pinto might have surprised us all in

some respects, but he had yet to perform in front of a noisy crowd, and that could make all the difference in his timing. Maybe Mrs. Nolly was only teasing me about jumping the Ragman.

We came back out of the woods and into a bright, crisp morning. The blanket of gray dawn which had lain over the show grounds was at last gone. Electricians working with the sound system produced a blare of static, then put on an album of fox trot music.

When we rounded the grandstand, the first person I saw was Mrs. Nolly. "Heigh-ho," she cried. "We've looked everywhere for you. Practice time; practice time!"

Behind her were Rusty on Beau, Suzanne on Jack, the twins on the twin sorrels, Toby on the filly Stogy, and Carver on a shined and polished Benny.

We rode up to the gate only to find Garson Gambill standing haughtily in front of it, blocking it.

He said, "I don't want to hear any mouth about this, now. As you can see, it's taken me half the morning to drive all these pesky riders out of here so I could turn my horses loose for a romp."

Mrs. Nolly fumed at that. "Garson Gambill, you know very well there are two perfectly good grazing pastures here — and you're just as welcome to use them as anybody else. What right do you have to close off the ring? I won't have it."

"Yeah? And just what do you think you're going to do about it, old woman?"

Carver whispered to me, "He's made a deadly mistake there," and backing Major several quick steps, Mrs. Nolly said just two words, "Heads up!"

She cantered Major straight for the gate, clearing it handily. Garson Gambill started to pick himself up out of the dust, but panicked when he saw the rest of us. He just ducked his head and hugged the ground.

Suzanne came next, setting the palomino off early for a long, low jump. Rusty was right behind her, then the twins. They jumped the gate shoulder to shoulder while Carver hung back, laughing atop his walker. Toby was too engrossed in a candy bar to take part, so I brought up the rear.

"That's giving it to him," someone yelled. There was wild clapping all around the ring. At least we weren't Garson Gambill's only enemies. Mrs. Nolly grinned like a piano keyboard as Gambill stalked away in anger.

Gambill's horses, on the other hand, were delighted to have company. They tore themselves away from the lush grass in the center of the ring and rushed about in fits of bucking and galloping.

Just then, Clus ambled up to ringside, several of his pups in tow. His helmet was tilted at its usual angle, and his pipe sent up spirals of dusty blue smoke. "It's going to rain tonight," he said around his pipe. "These aching old bones tell me so."

"Rain?" Carver Coy scoffed. "What do you take me for, an imbecile? Out of that beautiful blue sky will come *rain*? I've got old bones, too, old friend. And let me assure you, they predict sunshine. Loads and loads of clean, hot sunshine. Rain, my mother's hat! Rain, my foot!"

At five o'clock sharp, the rain came. And Uncle Clus was right there. "It's as I said," he crowed to Carver. "I told you so. I was right."

And it kept right on raining.

The Ragman was in excellent spirits. He seemed to welcome the mud, which deepened and rutted as more feet and hooves trod through it. As far as the eye could see, riders were decked out in plastic rain gear. They moved their horses slowly about to keep them from stiffening up in the chill.

Carver passed out his annual good luck charms, rings made by bending horseshoe nails. Workmen hauled the judges' stand to the center of the ring — a white wooden gazebo. It was barely big enough to hold the judge, the ringmaster, and the show secretary, much less the announcer with all his bulky equipment.

Static came on the sound system and the announcer cleared his throat.

"Ladies and gentlemen, it is my pleasure to welcome you to the thirty-fifth annual Highlands Charity Horse Show. Please clear the hunt field, riders. Local pleasure horses, get ready to show in the main arena."

I had made a bargain with Mrs. Nolly. If the Ragman reacted to the crowd all right, I would enter him in the first jumping class. He fidgeted beneath me and I gave his shoulder a pat to settle him down.

The horses moved into the ring at a trot. Ears up, the pinto blinked as the bigger horses passed him, but he kept to the rail and showed no ill temper when inexperienced riders reined in too close on his heels.

"Walk," called the announcer at the judge's instruction.

Behind the box seats stood the concession

stand manned by Dad and some of his friends. The money they made was for the hospital building fund, and when he waved at me his white shirt and apron stood out against the grayness of the morning. But he had customers and I had a class to ride. I really loved my Dad.

"Do yourself proud," said Mrs. Nolly, riding up beside me, talking out of the side of her mouth. "Remember to smile, darling. Pleasure horses are supposed to give pleasure, you know. You've got to look as if there's nothing you like better than a long wet ride in the mud," and off she went.

"Canter," called the ringmaster, and the Ragman moved smartly away. I eased him to the inside curve and passed Mrs. Nolly, who rode serenely with her left hand. She was probably right. She would, as usual, take first place.

The other riders came from local summer camps. They rode stiffly and forlornly, and they looked as though they would break like fragile little dolls.

The judge asked us to walk, reverse, and continue walking. I noticed he seemed to be looking at me, so I made an extra effort to look smart. I had been used to taking the trophy in classes Mrs. Nolly decided not to enter, but this was one of those times when I would have to ride for second place.

I finally caught sight of Rusty. Standing in the back of the exhibitors' box, he gave me the okay sign. We trotted a turn of the ring and then pushed into a canter from a trot — a fairly tricky thing for a novice to do right.

About that time, a crowd of camp horses passing the box seats bolted and one of the girls fell off into the mud. A walk was called while ring attendants rounded up the stray horse. The girl was all right, it turned out, and the crowd applauded for her.

A trot was called again and as the Ragman rounded the upper end of the ring, I found we were alone on the rail and getting the once-over from the judge. He marked something down on his notepad and looked at us again.

The camp riders kicked their horses hard to keep them going, then had to haul up on the reins to hold them back. Ahead, Mrs. Nolly was showing us all how it should be done.

Chapter Eleven

Fog that had begun to settle in the tree-tops lifted off into the smoky sky. The horses slogged along on the soggy ground as the riders awaited the call to line up for the judge's decision. And Garson Gambill could not have timed it better.

The Ragman was passing the exhibitors' box at a slow trot when out of the adjacent box came the little man, hissing and shrieking and dangling a long whip in the pinto's face. I tightened my knees as the little horse wheeled and reared in terror, but I was nearly thrown anyway.

Garson Gambill laughed loudly as I reined the Ragman around and faced him. I could hardly believe his viciousness. "I think it can safely be said that you're out of the ribbons this morning," he said, tipped his derby, and sloshed off in the direction of the stables.

What bothered me most was the fact that he had also practiced his little trick on the camp riders. The girl could have been hurt; the Ragman could have pulled up lame. But none of this mattered to Gambill. He was, as Carver had long insisted, a mean and vindictive man.

The judge was sorry about my "bobble," as he called it. "It was a fine show. I had you marked second. Sorry about the mess-up. It was really too bad." He stood there in the mud, his long raincoat billowing around him. I guess he hadn't seen Gambill's maneuver. Worse luck.

As predicted, Mrs. Nolly got first. Carver ran out to carry her trophy for her. Suzanne was second, and Toby pulled a surprise by winning third place, the yellow ribbon. But the Ragman looked thoroughly dejected. He sensed something was wrong. When we left the ring, he hung his head sorrowfully.

"I guess this means you won't be trying that jumper class," Mrs. Nolly said. "See how despicable Gambill can be. I wish I had the fifty dollars to post a complaint."

"Let it go," I said. Garson Gambill had just convinced me Mr. Ragman deserved the chance to see what he could do in the ring. If the jumps were too much for him in all the confusion of a horse show day, I'd pull him out and wait until next year.

Mrs. Nolly's apartment was full of wet people and dogs, hamburgers and milk cartons, and "soup, for anybody who wants it," Carver announced.

Everybody chattered endlessly about how he rode, how he felt, how he thought he'd do the next morning. Suzanne led three cheers for Toby, the only rider none of us thought had a chance.

"Thanks," said Toby, pressing his lips shyly over his braces.

Mrs. Nolly was especially excited about it. "You did just beautifully. You would have thought it was George Morris himself up on that little filly. How did you do it, Toby?"

"I just sat there," Toby said. "When the other horses trotted or cantered, so did Stogy. I knew I'd mess up, so I didn't do anything."

"Keep on doing that," she said. "You might luck out and place in the championship pleasure class Sunday afternoon."

Eva knocked at the screen door and paraded in, haughty as ever. "I couldn't believe it," She giggled. "Jiggsie's dad is wearing an apron and cooking hamburgers at the concession stand. Next thing we know, it'll be a family affair, with Jiggsie as Hotdog Queen." Mrs. Nolly was quick to reply.

"We should be grateful, Eva. If it weren't for volunteers like Mr. Jiggsen manning the concession stand, handling the parking, taking up the tickets, and selling the programs, why we wouldn't have much money for our local charities, would we?"

I was surprised to see that Eva could turn almost as red as Rusty could. I suddenly saw her as someone who, like a hurt little animal, strikes out at anybody who tries to come near.

Carver was irritable. "Let's change the subject, talk about birds and flowers, and about how one Carver Coy and his fine horse Benny are going to win the walking class. Yes, indeed. It'll be the spectacular Carver Coy, all decked out in his best suit, collecting the trophy."

"Win it for me," I said mournfully.

"I'm not worried in the least," he said. "But I have to have loads and loads of sunshine, so when the wind catches in my coattails, they blow back and show the bright red satin."

"It doesn't look like anything but more rain to me," I said.

Carver winked at me, and directed his attention to Clus, who was seated on the uncomfortable old couch with a gang of his dogs. "What do you say, my old friend?"

"Sunshine," Clus said.

"Dreamer," Carver snorted. "I may need sunshine, but do you mean to tell me you expect it to come out of that gray sky? What do you take me for, an imbecile?"

Clus said, "My bones say sunshine, and sunshine it'll be. My dogs could use some of that, too." Clus bent down to play with the mongrels and Carver started snorting again.

"Aye. He thinks I'm a total imbecile."

At one o'clock, the clouds swept away and the sun came out.

After lunch I worked hard on the Ragman's hooves, digging out the mud and gravel packed in the crevices around the frogs. He still seemed depressed about the morning and wasn't his usual gay and nippy self. I threw a fly sheet over his back and buckled the strap under his neck.

"You'll get your turn," I told him. He gave me a bored glance, sneezed, and rolled his eyes back.

Carver gave Benny a long workout behind the barn, and by the time the Tennessee Walkers were put on standby, Carver was feeling fit as a fiddle. The sun beaded on his forehead and reddened his nose, but he was a splendid sight in his freshly pressed habit, white shirt, and tie.

"I'm a beautiful sight," he told me.

Mrs. Nolly handed his battered old derby

up to him and began a conversation with the horse — "You is a good, good boy" — while Carver brushed the top of the hat on his forearm.

"Yes, sir, I feel really good about this one."

Benny looked far younger than his twelve years, and he liked the clean, sharp air left by the morning's rainfall. I tied red ribbons into the thin braids behind his ear while Mrs. Nolly called him "Sweety boy" and tickled his nose.

Carver had followed every rule of the Nolly Stables. Stirrups, bit, and buckles were spotlessly clean and the leather had a deep, rich sheen. The browband of the bridle was a smart red and beige check and the linen girth was so white, it looked new.

His clothes were pressed and clean, though the seams showed some wear, and his favorite number was on his back. Carver Coy was number one, and hoping the judge would see it that way.

Half a dozen Hackney ponies filed out of the ring and Carver led his class inside at a smooth running walk. Behind him came a tiny little girl on a big gray mare, and next, riding in his shirt sleeves, a trainer who was giving a colt his first day of sights and sounds as a budding show horse.

Clus stood his crutch against the railing and sat down with Mrs. Nolly in the front of the exhibitors' box. It was beginning to fill with Carver's fans and friends, and when his break came, Dad joined us. Garson Gambill was nowhere to be seen as the loudspeaker crackled and Carver's favorite song blared forth:

I got a ten dollar ring
And I feel like a king
On my Tennessee Walking horse.

"Look yonder," said Uncle Clus and we looked up to see Gambill and friends heading into the ring. Manhandling the roan stallion as it moved anxiously through the gate, Gambill wore a bright yellow saddle suit with matching boots and derby.

Each of his riders was decked out in matching ensembles. Number forty-seven was in forest green, number eighty-three wore royal blue, and number fifty-nine wore all black. The judge and ringmaster picked their way across the mud to the gazebo. The music went on and Benny fell into step with it as Carver began his act for the crowd.

Sitting back in the saddle, he tipped his hat to the spectators in the grandstand. He smiled, kept an even touch on the rein to get Benny on stride, then popped the hat back in place. The crowd cheered and clapped every time he passed, and old friends in the box seats yelled, "That's him, judge. That's him, number one."

"They're all making a nice show," Mrs. Nolly said. "It bothers me. Last year when Carver came in second to Gambill down in Raleigh, it nearly broke his heart. I felt so sorry for him."

"Well, just look at him now," Clus said. "He's bright as a new dollar."

At every turn of the ring, Carver drew applause. Gambill made the flashier show with his fine suit of clothes, but his set jaw and lowered head did nothing to endear him to the people. He looked so resentful. The announcer called a walk and Gambill cut his roan sharply in front of Benny. Benny slung his head unhappily.

At that, Mrs. Nolly shook her head angrily, but she said nothing.

"I was sorry to learn about your horse," Dad said to Eva. She had just dragged in from the hillside where she'd been watching the hunter class. "I don't know a great deal about horses, but I very much admire yours. He's very fine."

Eva thanked him quite nicely.

The music beat right along and the

entries moved at a rocking horse canter. It was Benny's best gait. He looked fast, although by staying at a collected pace, he didn't cover much ground at all. Some of the others were so down in the hips that they appeared to be reaching for the sun with their knees.

Five more turns of the ring and Mrs. Nolly said she couldn't stand the suspense a minute longer. "Why don't they line 'em up and see what a good animal looks like when it's stripped of its saddle."

The announcer must have heard her, for he called, "Grooms into the ring." A swarm of men and boys leapt over the gate or slipped through its slats. Carver nudged Benny's elbow joint with the toe of his boot so the horse would "park out." Hopping to the ground, he had the girth unbuckled by the time Rusty got there.

"I think you got it made," Rusty puffed, "no fooling." He slipped the saddle off and gave the big walker a quick rubdown with a grooming cloth. Benny lifted his head and perked his ears; the grooms stood by while the judge made his rounds, circling each horse, making notes, tipping his hat to the women. He took his time looking over Gambill's roan. He checked the scarred flesh above the horse's fetlocks and gave Gambill a disapproving look.

After he checked the little girl's gray horse, the judge approached Carver and Benny.

"Too bad," he said, marking a change in his notebook. "Did you happen to notice this? I'll have to mark you down for it. Your horse has swellings in his front legs."

Carver's face collapsed like a tent with its pegs pulled loose. "No sir, I honestly didn't."

"It doesn't look too serious, but its a matter of soundness. It might be a good idea if you were excused from the class, don't you think?"

"Wonder what could have happened?" Clus mused as Carver took off his hat and led Benny from the ring.

The results were: fifth place to the little girl on Top O' Morning, fourth place to the little miss on the gray, third place to the lady in black, second place to the boy on Dasher's Mate, and first place to the man in yellow: Mr. Garson Gambill. I couldn't understand how the judge overlooked the condition of Gambill's horse.

Carver Coy was crushed. Number one was clearly down and out.

Chapter Twelve

"He was right to pull me out," Carver said. "He was right."

He ran his fingers gently down the legs to Benny's swollen fetlocks.

"I'll help you with him," I said. "Whatever has to be done."

Carver grunted and heaved and got himself up from his bent-over position. "A good man with horses will keep a keen eye to the condition of an animal's legs. And he'll be a good deal sharper than I was. Do you feel any heat in those swellings?"

Rusty shook his head. "The rest of the leg is cool, too."

"Check the other one," I said.

"It's cool."

"What about the hooves? Heat in a hoof can tell you a great deal about a horse."

"I can't feel any," Rusty said. I checked the back ones. They weren't even puffy.

Carver was exasperated. "With all my years' experience in this business, I got a case of get-him-good last night, and now I'm paying for it. Get-him-good is when you decide that you need to work your horse a little extra — what difference does it make if it's the middle of the night? So you pile out of bed, saddle up the old boy, and work up and down this corridor that's practically as hard as concrete. I should have known better; I worked him too much.

"But no, I was so full of blue-ribbon nonsense that my get-him got the best of me. To think I might have done him some real damage. I left him standing in his stall and didn't even give him a rub. That's how addled I was."

I said, "But it didn't bother his hind legs."

"Yeah," Rusty said. "Chicken's right. Why wouldn't he have trouble in all four legs?"

"Because those hocks are marvelous shock absorbers, but up here in front, the only 'give' is below the fetlocks, so quite a bit of harm can be done, you see. All those tendons and ligaments are subject to great stresses and strains, and, of course, they're what connect muscle tissue to the bones so that there can be movement. But what did the judge know? Maybe he thought I worked Benny in short circles and got him bruised.

"I'm just one of a thousand riders that judge will see in a year's time. He doesn't care about all my good intentions. He just sees a couple of legs with swelling in them;

he knows that's bad management. So out I go.

"If I'd won that class, I'd have used the money to make a formal complaint against Gambill. And while I was at it, I could say I don't like his spick-and-span yellow suit and his big roan horse and his little sneaky eyes. Phooey on blue-ribbon fever. I'm beginning to think that at his age, Benny's earned his retirement from all this hullabaloo. And maybe old Carver Coy has too."

Rusty ran a body brush over Benny's slick neck. "Does the puffiness go away all by itself?"

"Oh, it likely will," Carver said. He didn't want to expand on the subject, so I did.

"Here, the legs should be rubbed upwards toward his heart. There's some congested blood there, and we ought to put pressure bandages on for the night."

Carver went on, "It's not an easy thing to have to leave an arena on foot at the order of a judge."

"I wish you wouldn't quit," I said. "You can beat Gambill. Benny's all right, and he's got too much spunk to be turned out to pasture."

"Let's just concentrate on bandaging him. Get some cotton and some wool and we'll wrap him snug below the knees all the way down to the coronet. That should put him right by morning."

I'd never thought of Carver Coy as a quitter. He was the one we all counted on for encouragement. Even Mrs. Nolly did. He always had a kind word for losers and winners alike, and if things didn't come out as planned, he'd usually say:

"Well, now, I've never thought it took any great fortitude to win. That's always been the easy thing to accept. It's a defeat that's so hard to take." And it was along those lines that Mrs. Nolly spoke to her captive audience late that afternoon.

"Sportsmanship, as all of you know, is an enthusiasm and participation in sport without expectation of victory and with the ability to accept defeat graciously, regardless of whether defeat comes from poor performance or from something unexpected — such as happened to Carver Coy here."

"I wish you wouldn't talk about me that way," he said.

Mrs. Nolly was in top form, strutting back and forth across her living room floor, which was again dotted with people and dogs. I gave Carver a sympathetic smile. He needed it.

"We must be better sports in the future," she said.

"How many of me are there?" Carver asked.

"Man and horse have been as one for centuries," she went on. "They've explored uncharted territories together, hunted for food together, gone into war together. And now they go into show rings together to give of their best insomuch as ability is admired and rewarded and the show horse judged against certain set standards of beauty and excellence."

"I don't see how she can talk so long without taking a breath," Carver said. "I'm a highly intelligent fellow, and you don't have to say long sentences to convince me that I'm in big trouble."

"I assure you that if I were to lose — if that could possibly happen — I would turn the other cheek," Mrs. Nolly said.

"I just wonder if you would," Carver replied.

"You're just afraid of losing to Garson Gambill again," she said.

"Nonsense. I am not!" Carver stormed.

"You are too. Don't you say you aren't when I know full well that you are!"

"Guess I'd better get myself on down to the judges' stand," Clus said, paying them no attention. "I wonder how I'll sound over the loud-speaker this year."

At least it was enough to stop their arguing before they could really get started, for every year the show secretary and the board of trustees let Clus say a few words at the end of the first day of the show. He did his thank-you's while the crowds continued their getting up and going, gathering up umbrellas and ponchos, show programs and children. We all went down to ringside to listen.

The people poured out of the grandstand and box seats in a steady stream, but Clus went on talking.

"In a year's time, hundreds of dogs and pups pass through the local animal shelter. Under the policy of our county board of commissioners, each dog is kept a minimum of ten days before it must be destroyed.

"This allows any suspected cases of rabies to be checked out in the event someone has been bitten. It also gives local citizens an opportunity to look over the animals and choose pets. However, Blowing Rock and the surrounding area is not a great deal different from other places. After a time, just about everybody is tending all the dogs he can. Some of my best customers have as many as three dogs they picked out at the shelter.

"The main road is getting to be impassable and our county needs money to rebuild it as well as for a program to educate people to the need for neutering pets they do not intend to breed or show professionally. This would mean an enormous reduction in the number of homeless and hungry animals loose on the countryside. It would bring to an end much needless suffering. And, for me, there would not be so much pain at having to take charge of the destruction of those that aren't chosen."

Clumps of people stood listening to Clus, and those who moved on toward their cars moved more slowly in order to hear.

"Of course," he said, "us retired folks have to do something, and I admit it's a pleasure helping the dogs find good homes. Our fluffy pups usually have no trouble at all striking people's heart strings, but it's a poor fellow, indeed, who ends up with the face of a German shepherd, the short little legs of a dachshund, and the long thick hair of a collie. Thank you," he said to a sprinkling of laughter. "He thanks you, too.

"So it's sort of a habit with me to hang around the barns every year to show off my dogs in the hopes someone will take an interest. In fact, I thought it was a stroke of genius this year when I brought all twenty-two of them with me. I wanted to get in everybody's way so they'd notice my little orphans.

"There we were," he told his attentive listeners, "when an owner-exhibitor name of Mr. Garson Gambill came flying out of nowhere on this great mare, scattering dogs every which way, and sending me sprawling on the ground. Well, naturally, some of the dogs took exception to this, partly because some of them think I'm their natural father — we're just that close. And partly because the big horse frightened them.

"So out of their fear, the way dogs will, they began to growl and snap, and about that time, the mare decided she'd had just about enough of being in the middle, and she wheeled and lunged and wheeled and lunged some more, and the next thing I know, Mr. Gambill has landed kaput right in the mud beside me. Him in his yellow suit and me in my old dungarees and jacket.

"Well, he gets up and chases his big horse back toward the stables and I figure that's pretty much the end of it.

"Within an hour, Mrs. Goldfine tells me

that she and the show steward had received a complaint from Mr. Gambill that my dogs constitute a hazard to the riders and I would have to return them to the pound during show hours. That's the very time I'd hoped to give them away. So I have to count on you people to come to me.

"I'm empowered by the county to accept your donations to our program. In fact, I could walk you over to the shelter. It's not really too far from here. I've gone on long enough, I guess, so I'll just thank you for your good time and attention and for anything you can do to help our little friends. Good evening."

Clus drew a standing ovation. Motorists with their windows rolled down added their horns to the clamor.

Mrs. Nolly and I went tripping over the mud to congratulate him. Carver was right behind us, and right behind him came Garson Gambill.

Gambill said, "I'll tell you one thing, Mr. Clus Jiggsen. You have humiliated me and belittled me to an extent I cannot, and will not, forgive. What do you have to say?"

"That my only intention was to tell the truth," Clus answered.

"I have been maligned and raised to public ridicule, and I have been laughed at," said Garson Gambill, raising his crop as though to hit Clus. "That's not a very good feeling!"

"I did not laugh when I told the story," Clus said. He flourished his hand to indicate the crowd and added, "They did."

"I intend to sue you for everything you can possibly beg, borrow, or steal."

Clus said, "I am not afraid. Age makes one less afraid, sometimes, and I haven't been malicious toward you as you have been toward me. If this evens up the score, so be it. If you want to sue me, then go ahead, if you care anything about some worn-out fishing gear, this old safari helmet I wear day and night, and my jar of old Mexican coins. Because that is all I have."

Gambill began to twitch and said, "I'll win suit against you and have your salary attached by the court."

"I have no salary," Clus said. "I'm a volunteer worker."

"You mean you fool around with those filthy dogs for free?" Gambill was livid now. He stamped his yellow boot in the mud.

Carver grabbed his chance while he could. "I wonder, Mr. Gambill, if while we're all assembled here and everything — if you'd give me a chance to tell you, man to man and face to face, exactly what I think of you."

"You might as well. Everybody else around here does."

Carver took a long breath. "Well, I don't like your spick-and-span yellow suit, or your big roan horse — though's it's certainly not his fault. And I don't like your little sneaky eyes."

Gambill said, "Go soak your head in a bucket of liniment," and stomped off in the direction of the barn.

"Oh, brother," Clus said. "That did me a world of good just hearing you say that."

"You bet," said Carver. "I feel like a new man."

Chapter Thirteen

The sunlight squeezed through a crack at the end of the earth and flooded away the last of the night. From a vast assembly of unseen woods creatures, it drew sounds of awakening. It lay like slippery saucers in the tops of buckets being brought up from the spring by stable boys; yet it was a hazy sun and it left gauzy, pale shadows behind horses and riders.

Mr. Ragman followed the rope in my hand and I followed Carver. It was the dawn of Friday morning and the closer we got to the jumping class, the more I began to think I was making a big mistake. The jumps stood like tombstones all over the ring. I'd never taken a really bad fall, but I knew that was because I'd never ridden a "green" horse over the big fences before.

"If I remember all this correctly," said Carver, "your first jump is to the right — this suspended rail."

"At least we start with something familiar to him," I said.

"Then you come to these parallel rails," he said, counting the pegs. "They're four feet high, and I'd guess the spread is another four feet. What would you do?"

"Pace him to go high and wide."

"All right, over here," and he crossed to the other side of the judges' stand. "You'll whip around the outside of the ring, cut sharply there, come up the grass to take this triple bar. Take him in close to it, is my advice. You have a six-foot spread, but your top bar is only four feet, six inches."

Only four feet, six inches. It has a big broad jump and it would cause many a good horse to be eliminated from the class, I was willing to bet. I retraced the course in my mind.

"Okay," I said, "I round the gazebo and come back down the grass and cross this hog's back, right?" This jump comprised a set of three rails, and spanned a width of five feet. The center rail, which stood higher than the two that flanked it, was four feet, nine inches. We proceeded to the last jump. It was a bar resting on a pair of orange blocks.

"This'll give most horses a fit, Elizabeth. There she lies, one foot off the ground. Most don't know what it is, and they certainly won't want to take it at a canter."

I led the Ragman up to the tiny barrier and he shied from it. He took a huge gulp of air through his nostrils and let it rattle out again. He put his nose down to the bar, then relaxed. Whatever it was, he had incorporated it into his world.

"Of course, it's a wonder you've got him in shape, using just those bits and pieces of jumps Mrs. Nolly has left over, but I think you'll do okay."

" 'Okay' won't be good enough in here," I said.

"I don't believe, given his temperament and your ability, there's a way to get you down in this show. I'm reminding you how much savvy the Ragman has to begin with."

"A lot you know; you're a walking horse man!"

"Elizabeth Jiggsen! I'll have you to know I've ridden bucking horses and jumping horses and prospected in the Utah desert in my time, and I'm not going to be put down by you. I know what I'm talking about."

I said to myself, Yeah, but you don't have to do the riding. Out loud I said, "Maybe I ought to wait until next year to show him in jumper. He's hardly shown in front of a crowd. He might get rattled."

"I hope he doesn't get as rattled as his rider. You're ghostly pale."

"I am not rattled."

"And I'm not Carver Coy and this here's not the Ragman, either."

"But he's never been over a hog's back before."

"Then why don't you just pop him over it, little one?"

Mr. Ragman was wearing only his halter, but I jumped up on his back anyway, backed him a few steps, and turned him to face the barrier. He cantered smoothly on the dew-wet grass, sprang from his hocks and went high and clean. He pounded on down the field and made a tremendous jump over the one-foot rail.

I rode back to Carver. "I guess I'm out of excuses now, but I still don't think we're ready."

And that was the truth.

Rusty came in early to help with the chores and even groomed the Ragman. That gave me a chance to get cleaned up in Mrs. Nolly's apartment and borrow some of Suzanne's riding clothes. I chose brown jodhpurs to match my boots and a yellow checked Ratcatcher shirt. That should do it.

By nine o'clock the sun was so intense women went about in hats made out of folded newspapers. Grooms hosed down the legs of animals just in from workouts. The total number of horses on the grounds had reached five hundred and fifty with the arrival of another jumper stable from Charlotte. Mrs. Nolly was off visiting with old friends, and Clus was, as usual, late. I looked everywhere for him but couldn't find him.

The grandstand was filled to capacity and some of its more enthusiastic occupants clapped and stamped their feet to hurry things along.

The announcer said his good morning, reminded everyone that program sales benefited the camp for handicapped children, introduced Judge Evelyn Carsells from Baltimore, and pointed out that the first event on the schedule was among the most exciting to be seen at any horse show. A cheer went up from the crowd. A minister blessed the horse show and the ringmaster drew a number from his hat.

I should have guessed the number would be forty: my number.

The Ragman didn't particularly like the crowd. It was one thing to be plodding along in a children's equitation class, or a pleasure horse class. But it was quite another thing to enter the ring on jumping day.

The second-deck box seats were filled with gaily dressed men and women, some of whom dangled over the rail to get a good look at us. I expected to hear laughter as I had in my dream, but there was none. I felt the Ragman skip beneath me, gave a firm pat to his neck, and turned him in a tight left-hand circle. This was it.

Tapping the top of my hunt cap for luck, I pulled the chin brace into place and let the Ragman canter strongly toward the suspended rail. He gathered himself, reached for the sky with his muzzle, and landed easily.

Only two strides away were the parallel rails. He planted his small hooves solidly in the soaked dirt and was moving slightly to the right when I guided him straight with the pressure of my knee. "Up, boy," I whispered along his neck, and the pinto picked himself up neatly, flew in a gentle arc, and came down effortlessly.

Working out the day before, he'd been a little sloppy behind, and that could cost valuable points. If a hind foot touched a barrier, it would call for half a fault. A front touch would count a whole fault, and knocking down a pole with the forefeet would be four faults against the horse.

A knockdown with the hind feet would mean an assessment of two points. And there were also penalties for first and second refusal of a jump, with third refusal eliminating the entry from competition. He — and I — would have to be careful and pay attention to the course. Getting carried away with the crowd could cause a serious accident.

The Ragman slung his head and cantered through a broad, shallow puddle which threw up a spray as we passed. He closed upon a gate topped by two poles, heaved up at my signal, passed over the uppermost pole with only inches to spare, and landed in a fit of bucking on the other side.

The crowd rallied to this exhibition of spirit. Next was a five-foot rail fence with brush piled on each side. It alone occupied the upper end of the ring, allowing riders plenty of time to get lined up on it, although the ring was so small and the pace so fast that it seemed the jump was on a curve rather than the straightaway.

This was a big jump, requiring height and distance all rolled into one. It would take speed, so I let the Ragman out a little. He bounded toward the jump, ignoring a side-line comment that "This pony'll never make it," took off eagerly, and made it over without any touches.

The footing was bad at the parallel rails, and they were deceptively broad. The Ragman straightened up quickly and picked up speed. "Go, go, go!" hooted a large woman in a red dress and shawl, and the Ragman did go. His hind legs corded as his hooves planted, and his front legs lifted and tucked like the landing gear of a jet on takeoff. I lay low along his neck, giving him his head so he could balance himself properly and make a good landing.

He proceeded with an air of amusement (his ears flicked back and forth) to the coop. Since it was only three feet, six inches high, he jumped it casually. I was surprised to hear a hind tick on the way down.

"Oh, Ragman," I moaned, but the crowd remained enthusiastic. They'd come to see jumpers and were delighted with this opening performance. I was less than delighted. The Ragman was a whole lot more secure about his jumping than I was. Popping over fences in the cool of the afternoon was one thing, but competing in the Highlands Horse Show was something altogether different.

I was breathing like a locomotive and the pinto was still as fresh as a flower. The closer we came to the end of the course, the greater the excitement of the crowd. It was like an electric charge that kept both of us going.

I relaxed my hands on the reins, and he eased off the pace. I let him canter almost to the end of the ring before turning him onto the grass.

The gate was hung with kibitzers shouting encouragement and advice: "That's a gal"; "Way to go, little one"; "Rein him in"; 'Let him out"; and "Yea, number forty!" That last one was Rusty, who'd been in a funny mood lately. No one was more willing to contribute time and effort to the cause of Mr. Ragman than Mr. Reinholt. But the contest was barely beginning. I rode on.

Ahead was the triple bar, the barrier made of three single rails placed one after the other. The first was the shortest, the second was of medium height, and the third was the tallest. The jump, as Carver had pointed out, spanned six feet, and I urged the pinto to pick up speed. He did so almost gratefully, as though cramped by the lack of space in the course.

He leaped it easily, seeming to hang for a second above the bars. Kneeling inside the judges' stand, the show photographer caught the moment on film, and the Ragman swung gracefully on, slinging his head in a show of fun.

I kept him on the grass, took a short right turn, and urged him on toward the hog's back. He made another long, high jump, and the crowd's ohs and ahs rose and fell as he approached the little one-foot jump at the end of the course.

He took a big healthy jump, clearing it by a couple of feet, and cantered out the gate to the roar of the spectators. I'd never heard anything like it. It sent chills over me. I couldn't believe we'd made it.

"Mr. Ragman, one-half fault," the announcer said, and the roar went up again louder than before.

Rusty loosened the pinto's girth and led him back and forth behind the box seats. "It looks good for you," he said, "but some of the men were saying they don't think the Ragman will be strong enough to stay in the competition.

"That's all I need," I said, panting to catch my breath. "Where's Carver?"

"Oh, fooling around over at the stable. He says he's not worried about you. He says you know what you're doing."

The second horse had a clean round until he crashed into the triple bar and went down. Screams went up from the stand, but it was the kind of accident many had come to see. Once the horse and rider got themselves up unhurt, there was applause. The jump crew reset the jump, the judge measured it to make sure every horse would face the exact same span, and the third horse entered the ring.

She was a flighty mare given to twisting her tail nervously as she approached a barrier, and she took a harrowing route across the three jumps next to the box seats. She came across the first one on the right, the second one on the left-hand side, and the third on the right again.

Her rider was a tall thin man who held his head to one side. He fought his horse all the way, bringing her up short into a bundle of energy, then releasing her into a frenzied flight toward the next obstacle. She was a very dangerous horse, but he rode her recklessly anyway, and the crowd went wild as she flashed toward the second set of parallel rails. She nearly sat down in the mud, but managed to regain her footing and took off at the last possible second. It seemed she would land in the middle of it, but somehow she got over, and in another frantic moment, she was careening out the gate. She'd picked up a half-fault on the hog's back. Her name was Wampum.

The next three horses floundered on the sodden track, the first two coming out with five points, and the third with two. A big solid horse named Regrets Only was the next to get by with half a point. Although he was a veteran jumper who had seen every barrier a thousand times before, he still took an interest in what he was doing.

Despite his hugeness, he moved well, and

the blonde woman on his back handled him almost lazily. They had between them the kind of trust I was beginning to feel for Mr. Ragman, but they had experience to boot. And that could make all the difference.

"Yoo-hoo, here I am," Mrs. Nolly called down from an upper box seat. "What a beautiful round, Elizabeth. Dear, this is Mr. Sidney Dailey, an old friend. He's very much interested in your Mr. Ragman — wants to buy him."

Mr. Dailey, who was expensively dressed, showed me an expansive smile and tipped his pale blue fedora. "I would like to buy Mr. Ragman," he said.

"Mr. Dailey owns Wampum," Mrs. Nolly said. "He's really serious, dear."

That barely registered. We were running back to the gate as the announcer repeated, "Number forty, please come into the arena for the jump-off." Rusty cinched up the girth and I took the Ragman into the ring at a feisty trot.

This would be it, I thought. The Ragman would be worn down by all the pressure and probably would collect a few points this time around. I decided to ride him lightly and let him go as he pleased. We began the round.

A gang of the Ragman's fans was raising

a happy ruckus at the top of the grandstand. He cleared the first barrier and sped on to the next.

Up and over it, he took the gate with lots of room to spare and galloped hard for the big brush and fence. It was almost as though he realized the need to build power for this one, and he skimmed it and made a graceful landing to a burst of applause.

He slipped on the curve, but kept going without giving it a second thought. The parallel rails passed under him and then the coop. He bounded over the triple bar, slowed his canter until he rounded the judges' stand, then sped over the hog's back in fine form. He skipped over the tiny suspended rail and was home free before I even knew what had happened.

"Mr. Ragman, no faults," came the announcement, and a thunder of hard clapping spilled down around us.

I couldn't believe it. The Ragman was starting to sweat in the heat of the day and I peeled off my hat and mopped at my face with a handkerchief. Then I put the cloth to good use around the pinto's ears and under the bridle straps.

Carver popped up beside me. "Well, with all this noise and suchlike, I figured I'd better get on over here and see what you were up to." He and Rusty ran body sponges over the little horse's flanks and legs.

A cheer went up when Wampum came into view. Her beauty had captured the admiration of the people, and her antics made for a hair-raising show. The mare burst over the barriers, slipped and skidded between them, flew to perilous heights, zoomed hither and yon with her rider flapping a crop along her neck and crying orders on every jump. Somehow they made it without any faults.

So did Regrets Only, plodding stoically around the course, hardly batting an eye.

The announcer explained the conditions of the last jump-off. Not only faults, but time as well, would count. If two horses tied with the same number of faults, the faster horse would be declared the winner. To give each rider an opportunity to line up on the first jump, the judge would start her stopwatch when the horse's forefeet left the ground at the first obstacle.

Mrs. Nolly arrived in a buzz of excitement.

"You know what to do," Carver said.

"Let him out," said Rusty.

"Hold him in," said Mrs. Nolly.

Everybody had his own idea, but the riding was up to me alone. I knew if we were to remain in the money against a horse as fast as Wampum, we would have to cut all the corners possible. But there was danger in riding too hard, especially now that the soft ground was so deeply pitted. The prospect of causing the Ragman a fall frightened me, because the horses often came out of falls worse off than their riders.

Speed also might mean bungling too many of the jumps. I made my decision and we started the round.

The Ragman jumped smoothly, his big heart seeing him over the trying course for the third time in a row. He pricked his ears at each barrier, then swiftly made short work of it.

"Go!" screamed the lady in red. I could see her flailing her arms in the grandstand. The Ragman lifted off and was clear of the fourth jump. When he was safely over the parallel rails and the coop, I slowed him abruptly and turned him onto the grass.

Chapter Fourteen

Two strides later, he sailed over the triple bar. We slowed again in a sharp turn and then bounded toward the big hog's back. On the way up, he drew a front tick and when we dashed out the gate, the announcer said "Mr. Ragman, front touch, one fault."

Carver was beaming. "Good ride. You made a wise decision. He went the round in good time."

The clapping died down, and Wampum flashed past us at a gallop, her rider sawing at her mouth and cursing under his breath. The first three jumps brought screams from the stand, and the mare took a half fault on the brush and fence.

She slipped and slid her way onward, cleared the rails by an impressive margin, landed with a splat, and drew another half fault with a badly timed jump of the coop. She was headed into the triple bar when she planted her hooves and refused.

"That earned her three faults right there," Carver said. "It's that rider of hers anyway; he's made a nervous wreck out of her."

Wampum refused a second time, quivering and bolting to the side when her rider tried to bring her around. On the third refusal, she was eliminated from the competition.

"Close call," Mrs. Nolly chuckled. "She's a pretty good horse, even in the wrong hands."

Someone said, "You're it."

I turned to find the blonde woman grinning at me. "I'm not chancing a fall on that track. Besides, this boy is too big to move very fast."

She stepped into the stirrup and pulled herself up into the saddle. Then she rode him just as she said — at a slow, even, unexciting pace. The big horse eased himself over each barrier, picked up a fault when he stumbled at the last and smallest of the jumps, and did it all in a total of fifty-five seconds.

"The winner," said the announcer, "Elizabeth Mae Jiggsen's Mr. Ragman, time forty-one seconds."

Carver said, "Now, who was it who wasn't going to have anything to do with this ugly old pinto pony?"

It was a big golden trophy with a jumping horse mounted on top, but not a chunky, blocky pinto jumping horse who sneezed and rolled his glass eyes. A jumping horse more like Wampum, or a cross between Wampum and Regrets Only.

I was still painfully aware of the differences between Mr. Ragman and the well-bred animals at the Highlands Charity Horse Show. In the back of my mind, I could see myself decked out as Annie Oakley — black felt cowgirl hat, fringed gloves, guns shoved down into a holster, pointed-toe cowboy boots — leading my little pony around the show grounds.

Instead, people stopped to congratulate me. I was having trouble seeing Mr. Ragman as my dream horse, but when people smiled and said they had never realized ponies could jump as high as horses, I calmly replied that the Ragman wasn't a pony, although at fourteen hands, three inches, he almost was.

Eva was mysteriously absent, having gone home to pout according to Toby, who got it straight from his mother. The twins hung around the tack room to answer the phone and say no, there weren't any horses for rent during the show.

I exercised Major for Mrs. Nolly, watched Rusty take a third place in hunter equitation, helped Suzanne switch Jack's bit from a Mullen Mouth Pelham Bit to a lightweight snaffle. It was easier on the Palomino's sensitive mouth and he settled right down.

Toby was being careful who he spoke to, now that he was a big winner, and there was just a hint of a swagger about his walk. And, when the last of Friday's classes was over and done, I was still being pursued by Mr. Sidney Dailey.

He found me sitting atop a fence rail, watching a girl work a big-boned hunter through a figure eight at a canter.

He said the magic words: "With eight hundred dollars, you could have a horse like that."

I sulked. I said, "The Ragman's not worth eight hundred dollars."

"Not to you, maybe, but to me, yes. If you don't think he's worth that, why don't you go ahead and sell him to me?"

"I don't mean I think he's worthless."

"Maybe a thousand dollars would suit you better. I've had my fill of the fractious, uncontrollable horses. What I need is a good-tempered, strong little horse with the will to win big."

"But he's only a pinto," I heard myself say.

"I don't care if he's a zebra, as long as he

jumps the way he did today," said Mr. Dailey. "But, here, don't let me get too pushy, Miss Jiggsen. I'll tell you what. There's still tomorrow and Sunday. Give some thought to my offer. You can let me know later." He tipped his hat in a good-bye way.

At the barn, I took a nap on a bale of hay and let the smells and sounds of the stable waft over me. I heard Clus tell again what a good day he'd had: Six dogs with new homes, and almost three hundred dollars in donations. I took care of my allotment of chores and was so preoccupied with my thoughts that I barely spoke to Carver and Rusty.

I bandaged the Ragman's legs for the night and listened almost until eleven o'clock to Mrs. Nolly and the kids going through spirited renditions of "Carolina Moon" and "Yes Sir, That's My Baby" and so many others that I lost count of them.

Toby sang in a loud monotone and I was relieved when they all settled down and climbed into their sleeping bags for a long summer's night of sleep. I hung wearily over the Ragman's stall door. He stood quietly in his bed of deep straw.

I reached over, gave his ear a playful twist, and said: "One thousand dollars."

Saturday was a gray-sky day, muggier than Friday had been, and riders went about with sleeves rolled up and collars open. They worked steadily, but not for such long periods of time.

A night of warm, constant wind had dried out the track considerably and it was dragged and smoothed before the jumps were put in place. Fifteen numbers were drawn for line-up in the open jumper class, and as luck would have it, I wound up last.

This would mean more than an hour in the saddle awaiting my turn. But it also would be a chance to study the successes and mistakes of those who preceded me.

Judge Carsells had done herself proud this time. She had designed one of the most difficult courses a jumper can face. It was six barriers, every one identical except for the fact that each was slightly higher than the one before.

One thing was certain. I'd have to ride the Ragman high and wide to get him over such formidable obstacles. Mrs. Nolly had a right to her opinion — "Don't give it a passing thought, dear" — but I wondered if this would not be the end for number forty.

The poles were put one above the other, straight up and down. The first was an even four feet high — exactly the height the Ragman first jumped only a month earlier. The second was four feet, three inches; the third stood at four feet, six inches; the fourth at four feet, nine inches; the fifth at five feet; and the sixth at five feet, three inches.

Rusty couldn't understand the set-up. On other six-barrier courses he'd seen, the final jump was always five feet, not five-three. Well, I couldn't worry about that now.

The show ground was as warm with horses and people. Children went about in noisy clumps, asking to pat the show ponies and being told over and over to stand clear of their heels. There were smartly dressed women, workmen in overalls, fry cooks in aprons, horse dealers who studied prospects through squinting eyes.

And there were cowboys and grooms, highbred dogs on leashes, gaited horses whose long tails were tied up to keep them from dragging in the dirt.

The first class of the day was finally announced. The early arrivals bowed their heads for the prayer, then applauded as a tiny flag atop the judges' stand was hoisted. I felt light-headed and decided to pretend it wasn't me at all going into this class with the professionals.

The first horse out was the popular Regrets Only, who nodded his head in rhythm with the beat of his hooves and hardly noticed the barriers until he was virtually upon them. His large thick ears would flick forward, he would draw himself together, lift off, and float down safely on the other side.

He was fine until the last jump. Then he dragged down a pole and collected four faults.

No sooner was the barrier reset than a flashy stallion called Mr. MacIntosh trotted into the ring, wheeled and backed, then reared and fell onto the gate just as it was closing. Neither he nor his stunned rider was hurt, but Mr. MacIntosh had made his point. He did not intend to jump today, period. Carpenters were called to fix the splintered gate.

Wampum proved to be her usual flighty self, but she came off the fourth fence with only half a fault against her. Appearing self-assured as she approached the fifth barrier, she suddenly began to flounder. She pushed off hesitantly and it cost her four more faults. Her rider rode hard toward the last one and Wampum sprang in terror. There was a cry of relief from the grandstand.

Then when a mare named Maudie stumbled and fell at the first jump, the crowd leaped to its feet. The mare was led away by her rider, a dark-haired boy who limped from the fall.

Next came Sure-Fire, a gelding of extraordinary style and ability, who seemed a sure bet to clear the course. The third jump turned out to be his Waterloo. Sure-Fire dragged down three poles with his hind legs, and Judge Carsells recorded six points opposite his name.

One more horse remained to take the course before the Ragman. He was a race-horse-turned-jumper and every bit of eighteen hands high. He was snow white with a black muzzle and when he headed into a jump, he stood back a good twenty feet, clearing the rails at a daring height. On sucessive jumps, he stood back even further, barely getting his balance coming off one before he scrambled over the next one. They called him Army Man. "He can't keep it up," Carver predicted, and he was right.

The people howled as the powerful horse crashed through the fifth fence, sending his rider rolling across the ground amid the broken poles.

"They may have spoiled him," I said. It made me shudder.

And Carver answered darkly, "Could be they have."

Ring attendants caught Army Man handily and the ringmaster helped the rider up. "Nothing hurt but his pride," the announcer boomed, and the spectators clapped. Army Man seemed stiff in his right knee.

We were next and I was beginning to feel weak-kneed myself. Friends and acquaintances gathered around and I wondered if it showed.

"I still say this is good competition to lose to," said Carver.

"You would say any competition is good competition to lose to," said Mrs. Nolly. "That's what losers and quitters say. Now here's a winner, Go get 'em, Elizabeth."

The way I looked down at Rusty made him laugh. "Take care, Chicken."

I took up the reins and heard Carver bark at Mrs. Nolly. "I am not either a quitter."

Toby patted the Ragman's nose for luck and the others added words of encouragement. Nearby stood the persistent Mr. Sidney Dailey.

A hurrah went up for the last and smallest horse, a pinto who to most people seemed the least likely contender for a prize in open jumping. But he had earned a following the others had not. They chanted his name, they clapped and hooted. They had to be quieted down.

"Please . . . ladies and gentlemen," said the announcer.

An awesome silence followed. Through it cantered the Ragman, full of oomph and vigor, eager to see what lay in store for him. Into it came I, mired up in the peculiar slow-motion time an open rider experiences. My total attention was on the movement beneath me.

I decided to take him over the first obstacle slowly. His strong back legs thrust and he was easily aloft. Once down, I gathered him for the sprint to the next one. Sensing the urgency, he raised his tail slightly and took off. It was an effortless, clean jump, and it brought squeals of enthusiasm from the sidelines.

Now for the four-foot, six-inch pole. Tightening my knees, I drove my hands forward to put slack in the reins: "Careful, Ragman." He bounded, clean and high once again, slowed in the curve of the track, then showed some speed going into the big four-foot-nine jump.

As he rose into the air, his forefeet tucked to clear the rail; when his extended hind feet drew in for the landing, no ticks were heard. Two more to go, with the hot air bringing sweat out on both of us.

Five feet was the highest Ragman had jumped. His ears darted, his nostrils rattled with air, and he soared above it. And now, with one more remaining, the Ragman lunged at the huge barrier, sensing what great power he would have to summon to get over it. But he had it in reserve, well guarded by his good temperament. Nervous horses like Wampum spent their strength in bursts, unable to produce a steady performance when needed.

The Ragman took flight and it was all over. He had taken the course clean, and as the only jumper to do so, he would collect his second trophy in as many classes. His fans set up a real row, beating their hands and stamping their feet in hearty approval.

I rode for the gate but suddenly was overcome by the feeling that I hadn't ridden the course at all. The Ragman had taken everything in hand and I felt ashamed to be taking part of the credit. He was inexperienced and green, yet he had outjumped and outmaneuvered all the others. He answered a pat between the ears with a sling of his head.

Dad helped me down, saving, "You're pale, my girl, I hope you aren't overdoing it."

We walked along together. I didn't want him to know how scared I'd been.

Chapter Fifteen

Mother was spellbound.

Dressed in his gamy fisherman's outfit, Uncle Clus was settled loosely into a rickety lawn chair back of the box seats. To either side of him stretched booth after booth offering the best work of North Carolina artists. The judges had come and gone, leaving ribbons on the work they liked best, and while Marie Jiggsen was not among the winners, Clus was there to see that she didn't wind up among the losers, either.

"That two with a dash after it," inquired a matron in a cotton sun dress. "Does that mean twenty dollars?"

"Hardly, madam," said Clus. He eyed her sternly. "It was only at great length and after a good deal of argument that I was able to persuade the artist to part with this piece for the sum of two hundred dollars."

"It's not framed," the woman remarked, looking closely at the landscape.

"It's been our experience," Clus countered, "that customers prefer to have their own framing done to fit in with their decor. At the same time, they save the added expense of a frame which must be discarded."

The woman, evidently charmed by the oil painting and its craggy salesman, said "I think I'll take it. And that one over there, too."

Clus said, "The artist has kindly offered to contribute fifty percent of her earnings to our county dog pound."

"In that case, I'll also take the little one with the pinks and blues. It would be darling for hanging in an upstairs nook, don't you think so, Erma?"

The thin woman did think so, and she bought two more of Marie Jiggsen's works, one in watercolors and one in oils.

Dad and I were equally spellbound at the brisk trading taking place in the Jiggsen booth.

"You brought nearly all those old things I put away years ago," Mother said.

"I did," said Dad, "because I wanted the

people to have a good choice. And Clus and I especially wanted you, for once, to see your talent in the favorable light in which others see it."

"I'm just so overcome," she said. "I had decided not to ever enter a contest, as you very well know. So, look. I got entered anyhow."

She hugged Dad. The tight lines were gone from her mouth. There was luster in her eyes. This was the outlet Dad always insisted she needed.

Mother turned and gave me a hug. "I was so proud of you; I was so frightened. Your Mr. Ragman is turning out to be a very important fellow around here. And I'm so happy for you."

Standing at rope's end behind us, the Ragman dropped his head and grazed lazily at a tuft of grass. It was his first art show and he wasn't overly impressed, although there was a nice piece here and there. His glass eyes stared for a moment at all the bright colors. Then he snorted and chewed and waited for what was to come next.

Wandering back to the barn, I watched as the willowy Thoroughbreds moved back and forth, responding to the unseen commands of their masters. They skimmed over split rail fences, glided over water hazards and ditches, their every muscle and bone perfectly placed.

Their shoulders sloped strongly, hooves were small and hard and sure; eyes were large and bright, and chests deep and broad. Their coats were so finely groomed that every hair was in place.

The sky shook with thunder, the sun burst free of the clouds, and I was deep in thought.

In the main ring, junior three-gaited horses were going through their paces. Up and down the road behind the grandstand went walkers and roadsters, five-gaited horses tossing their heads and fretting at the bits, and cart ponies with such springy trots that they virtually walked on a cushion of air.

Hunters took their turns over the hunt field jumps, an occasional spill sending onlookers into fits. At the water hazard nearest the judges' post, a heavyset man came tumbling off after losing a stirrup. Spectators flooded onto the course as he thrashed about in the water and his horse went galloping on without him.

"Clear the course!" had to be repeated several times by the steward holding the megaphone. He attended the three judges who sat somberly at mid-field, score cards and binoculars at the ready, and he was annoyed that so much confusion could result from a simple fall.

All these things could be seen from Mrs. Nolly's sun deck at the barn. She had invited Sidney Dailey to have his say once and for all, and Mr. Dailey had brought along his brother, Leroy, who sported a chartreuse suit. Rusty and Carver were tending to the Ragman, and that left me to fend for myself. It made me nervous.

"One thousand, five hundred dollars," said Mr. Dailey.

"I told you her eyes would get big at that," Mrs. Nolly chuckled.

"Your Mr. Ragman is a hardy, plucky little fellow," he went on, "and my brother here agrees that he can go far, as well as high, in professional shows."

"He's won me over, I admit," said Leroy Dailey. He had very dark brown eyes which flickered from me to the arena and back again as he talked.

"The fact is, he's probably worth more than my brother is offering you. I myself would prize owning him."

Mrs. Nolly gave his credentials. "Mr.

Dailey is a member of the board of directors of the National Association of Exhibitors and Owners, and he owns a number of horses that are shown every year in Madison Square Garden in New York."

"I've been very fortunate," the elder Mr. Dailey smiled, "and since I'm getting rather old and on the heavy side, I'm taking the opportunity to coach a good many young people into fine, polished riders. I must say your work with this pinto of yours has been an inspiration to see. I wondered about your going into the jumps so loose-reined, but you evidently know what works."

"I had a good horse under me," I heard myself say.

"One thousand, five hundred dollars is a lot of money," the younger Mr. Dailey reminded everyone.

"It's probably a fair price," his brother said, "considering how new he is to the ring, but I'd venture to say he could double and triple his worth, maybe even go to the top. A season on the show circuit from Atlanta, Georgia, to the Northeast can be a real experience for a young girl — a demanding one, I can say that — and one you would treasure for the rest of your life."

"It might even lead to the Olympics," said Mrs. Nolly.

"It did for Molly Aspen."

"She was one of your riders?" I asked.

Leroy Dailey nodded proudly. "We keep a relatively small string of hunters and jumpers, ten to twelve at most, and a crew of five or six young riders who travel in the company of my wife and me. It's sort of on the order of a big family, but there's a lot of work to it."

"Elizabeth is a real worker," Mrs. Nolly said.

"Well, next year we're going to take a couple of Sidney's horses along to see what they can do. I imagine that would mean re-training his mare, Wampum, from the ground up. She's badly shaken, poor girl."

"Oh, Starsky's a good enough man," his brother put in, "but Wampum's too much horse for him. I'm letting him go after the show."

"I'm glad to hear that," Leroy Dailey said.

"So'm I," said Mrs. Nolly. "He couldn't do worse if he tried."

"So I had in mind Miss Jiggsen's taking her over, of course continuing to ride Mr. Ragman, too. And I've a young gelding name Seconds Please that I'd like to put in her hands."

Those were my hands he was talking about.

"You could bank your money and make a

decision later about investing in a blooded animal, if that's really what you want."

A blooded animal, I thought.

"Well, now," he said, seeing my expression of puzzlement, "don't let us push you, Miss Jiggsen. You'll need to think this through and decide what's in your best interests. We can get together later on and you can let us know something then."

Mrs. Nolly thanked them for coming by. I numbly added my thanks.

"Oh, don't let me leave without telling you the news," said the man in chartreuse. "Since the Highlands Horse Show is accredited by our Association of Exhibitors and Owners, we're empowering the show's three veterinarians to conduct tests to see if drugs have been used on any of the horses."

Mrs. Nolly said, "I understand Garson Gambill's stable is on the list."

"That's right, and mainly, I might add, because of requests from other exhibitors of walking horses. They put up the fee and posted the formal complaint last night."

"That'll please Carver," I said.

"Naturally, he told us where to go. He said that even if we did find that his horses had been drugged, he'd like to know what we could do about it."

We said our thanks again, shook hands with the two men, and they left.

Mrs. Nolly let it soak in, then she said, "It's an extravagant offer they're making you, Elizabeth, especially in these days and times. To be gone part of the year, you'd have to make special arrangements about your schooling, but I rather think your mom and pop would let you do it."

"I just can't believe what he said."

"It would be wonderful if you could do it, my dear. Now. Look at you. First you cry because you can't have what you want. Now you cry because you can have everything you want, and a good deal more."

Everything was spinning around. Clus in his hip waders. Dad in his aprons, Eva in her sunny curls, Mom at her easel, the Olympics, Molly Aspen: Elizabeth Mae Jiggsen.

And the Ragman.

And Rusty, even if he didn't know I existed.

"I got something in my eye," I said.

"So will I," Mrs. Nolly said, "if you don't take the Daileys up on their marvelous offer."

"Oh, I probably will," I said airily.

And Mrs. Nolly suddenly got something in her eye, too.

Chapter Sixteen

"He's not even funny about his feed," Carver said.

And Rusty said, "Except that he'd like to eat about a ton of it a day."

The Ragman buried his nose in his feed box, eating contentedly.

"Most jumpers I've had anything to do with get a little testy and peevish at show time. Not him. There he stands, solid as a rock. Doesn't even bother to switch his tail at flies. Darndest animal I've ever seen. When he came here, you'd be lucky to get a hundred dollars for him. Now I hear the price has suddenly gone up."

I turned my attention to the block of light at the end of the cool breezeway. Beyond, they were setting up a "touch and out" course, so called because a single tick would cause the horse to be eliminated.

Judge Carsells had made it a course requiring stamina. She had arranged six jumps, three on either side of the ring, and all six were triple-bar barriers. Entrants would be required to take the course twice, for a total of twelve jumps.

The spacing was somewhat better, this

being proved mainly by the ease with which the oversized Regrets Only made his way across the fences. He went clean as a whistle, emerging from the ring barely ruffled. Soon it was my turn.

The Ragman went the course with equal ease, going high and clean and keeping a smooth pace — something I'd particularly worked on. By this time, the pinto's supremacy over the big jumps came as no surprise to anyone. He had made believers out of all the doubters and took pleasure in the amount of applause that came storming down upon him.

The competitors here came in all sizes, weights, and colors. The only objective of open jumping was to get over the obstacles with as few faults as possible. Conformation and breeding were not what mattered over these big fences. The name of the game was performance, and the Ragman was as good as any of them — better than most.

"Aye, but what class you've got, my little man." Carver and the pinto had had an enormous liking for each other from the very start. "Who was good to you when certain persons — who shall be nameless — didn't think you had sense enough to put one foot in front of the other?"

Carver tickled his chin, and the Ragman bobbed his head vigorously in agreement.

Judge Carsells instructed the jump crew to clear the track next to the box seats and set up a gate with three bars above it. The top peg was put at five feet, six inches. "Uh oh," said Carver.

Staring at the enormous fence, I felt trembly.

"He's never faced anything that high," I told Carver.

"Putting him in the vast majority, I'd say," he answered. "You could forfeit, if you think it's asking too much of him."

Rusty just looked away, making no comment.

"I want to do it," I said.

"I'll not hear of it if you're only making a show for the Dailey brothers. It might be fairer to let the Ragman try this at some other time. Without all this pressure on him, you know."

"We'd both have to try it sooner or later, I guess."

"No guessing on this, now. Be sure of yourself."

Judge Carsells flipped a coin; number forty was up first.

The fence grew larger as we closed upon it. The Ragman raised his head in astonishment, then thrust it forward eagerly. I knew I would have to stick like glue over this one, or chance being left behind like a beginner. I felt the color and heat begin to drain from my face. Then he was airborne, a high-flying arc of horseflesh that cleared the top pole with inches to spare.

A roar went up from a crowd that couldn't believe what the little pinto had just done. I raised my hand, waving to them, and the sound was almost deafening. The Jiggsens, having joined Mrs. Nolly in the Daileys' box, clapped and fluttered, bending first to one side and then the other, making sure everyone knew, "That's our little girl; that's our little girl."

Regrets Only was yet to go and he appeared to be in top form as the blonde woman guided him through the gate and into a lazy circle to the left.

I slid down from the saddle and felt my knees give under me. It might not have put a dent in the Ragman, but it was the biggest fence of my life. "I know," I said to Rusty and Carver, "I'm as white as a sheet."

At just that moment, Regrets Only plowed into the sky, his powerful frame striving to get him clear, his small rider low to his thick neck.

"I think he's pulled a pole," Carver

shrieked, but he hadn't. The giant hind hooves, taking their good time about it, flipped up and over, and down he came. He stumbled, almost fell.

His rider shook her head back and forth, back and forth. She took off her hunt cap and fanned at her face with it. She slowed the heavy horse to a trot and finally to a walk. He came lumbering out the gate and stopped.

The blonde woman smiled at me and put her cap back on. "This old boy is no more up to that kind of fence today than I am. It's yours with blessings, Miss Jiggsen. I forfeit." And with that, I was the winner.

"If you enter the championship tomorrow," the blonde continued, "I'm certain you'll get the trophy. You've got me outpointed, and I think you've done a remarkable job. I wasn't counting on a horse like the Ragman."

"Me either," I smiled.

"Hello, Mr. Coy."

"Miss Merriwell," he said — and as she rode away, "Milo Merriwell's eldest daughter, my dear, that's who. Aye, you've ridden against the best today. You'll not do much better than that, no matter where you go. And that includes New York City."

I led the Ragman into the ring to collect

the trophy and blue ribbon. A tiny girl in a lacy white dress was doing the honors. The ringmaster stood by to assist her in handing over the big silver bowl, and the Ragman danced around at the end of the reins, resisting my patient tugs to bring him under control.

That's when the audience got to its feet and gave us a standing ovation, something rarely accorded a horse and rider, the local newspaper later would remark, and something seldom seen at any horse show, for that matter.

This settled it in my mind. I knew what I wanted now, and at the proper time, I would tell everyone.

The applause, as if to confirm my decision, went on and on. The Ragman shied about like a mischievous colt.

Duffy Dolittle, the show photographer, tacked up his sample photographs on the side of Mrs. Nolly's barn and did a banner business as riders came and went throughout the day. Even strangers were buying pictures of me and the Ragman. Business was grand.

Suzanne was doing her share to represent the Nolly Stables. That morning, she won a red ribbon for hunter seat equitation over fences, and in the afternoon she traded the

Palomino for the old bay, King, who carried her to first place in equitation, ages fourteen and under.

The Bledsoe twins were right behind her, earning second and third places, and Rusty spent his spare time helping a little boy with his saddle seat equitation.

Mrs. Nolly continued to egg Carver on about retiring Benny. "It's not Benny you're retiring," she said, "it's you."

"Maybe so," he said tiredly, "maybe so."

"Maybe, my foot! I *know* so!"

Mother went downtown to get more art supplies. Clus had sold her out, earning hundreds of dollars in the process. A few boys and girls were lined up, waiting to hike down to the shelter to select pets.

Eva sent word she would be there the next day, would be willing to show Spots in the hunter class — that she didn't really want to, but would, if that's what would make everybody happy. "She's her usual friendly self," was Rusty's comment.

Then it was his turn to rise and shine in the name of Mrs. Nolly and good sportsmanship. Carver pressed his coat for him and borrowed a pair of goggles to take the place of the ones Rusty had misplaced. He would be riding without a hunting bat or crop, because Mrs. Nolly preferred it that way, and always scoffed when she saw "overweight fools batting their horses to death to get them over a jump."

She'd cautioned her riders time after time that judges took off points for riders having to rely on spurs and whips in performance classes. "You got it or you don't," she said.

Toby strapped a sandwich box to the dee rings of Rusty's saddle and all was in readiness. The conformation hunter class would test Rusty for his ability to pace the big horse over the difficult course and would test the horse, Beau's Bonnet, for his style and endurance.

Seventy-five entrants would take the jumps. From this number the judges would choose twelve for conformation judging, taking into account the shape and line and stature of each Thoroughbred in turn. The winners would be selected on the basis of their good looks as well as ability.

Every manner of horse was seen that day. Lanky young hunters carrying their heads too high before a fence to make graceful jumps, children's horses poorly schooled and tending to race at the obstacles at the last minute, hard-mouthed horses seizing the bit and bolting off course, soft-mouthed horses who moved jerkily under their riders' unsteady hands.

And there were the well-trained, well-handled animals, self-confident, placed properly at each jump and hazard, unspoiled and alert and in fine condition. You could tell after the first few strides what chances an entry had. It became a betting game in which spectators marked down their favorites and argued among themselves as to the good points and bad points being displayed.

The hunt field itself was steep and rocky going, and its gray weathered fences were the same as they always had been: a sequence of split rail fences four feet high — six to the right, six to the left — and a pool of water twelve feet in diameter lying between. Trouble here usually resulted when riders gave their mounts too little rein on the downhill approach. Some simply balked at it and were eliminated.

By the time Rusty reached the hazard, he and Beau's Bonnet had made each fence look easier than the last. Beau's slim legs covered ground in long, unfaltering strides and he made a huge jump of the water, which he didn't like. It lay there, glassy and silver to his eye and of an unknown depth. He made certain he didn't touch it.

Thick patches of yellow and white flowers

colored the course. In complete control, reins held low and kept well separated, Rusty rode with no more concern than if he were out for an afternoon gallop. He seemed totally oblivious of the hundreds of people watching him.

"I like to see that boy ride," said Mrs. Nolly, seated comfortably in the grass beside me. "He sits as nice a seat as I've seen, present company excepted, of course."

"Beau has a good chance, doesn't he?"

"Ah, now, that Beau. He's a standout."

The judges thought so, too.

"See?" said Mrs. Nolly as we walked down the hill to where the judges were instructing the riders to untack and groom their horses. Mrs. Nolly waddled along, holding her broken arm, and recognized the tallest of the judges as her friend, Roscoe.

She called his name loudly and when he turned, she said, "Now, don't you go marking Beau down because you're mad." She kept on going toward the barn, talking in a voice loud enough for everyone to hear. "He's mad because he tried to buy Beau from me last winter down in Pinehurst, and I wasn't having any of it."

"Mrs. Nolly," I whispered, trying to quiet her down.

"Oh, I'm not afraid of judges, my dear.

They're only people. What would we do without them? Well, we wouldn't have horse shows, for one thing. But I mean, why should we be afraid of them? Judges get lonely at shows, you ought to at least talk to one once in awhile.

"Nobody ever forgives them," she went on at the top of her lungs. "The only happy people are the ones with trophies. The ones with the ribbons think they should have gotten the trophy; the ones without anything at all think they should have been in the ribbons. It's always been that way, and I don't see any chance of its changing.

"They've got to do whatever seems right at the time. Not every man and woman sees horses alike, you know. I knew a woman one time who never placed anything in a hunter class but bays, all because as a child she'd owned a big bay work horse and learned to ride on him.

"All kinds of things enter into a judge's decision. The main thing is learning to accept defeat as a challenge to do better next time around. It's as simple as that."

It was one of her longest sportsmanship speeches, but I didn't complain. If ever there was a time for it, it was horse show time. Mrs. Nolly proceeded to the barn where Toby had nailed up an eight-by-ten glossy of him riding Stogy in the pleasure horse class.

I returned to the hunt field to see Rusty take a third-place ribbon and to hear him say, characteristically, that he was happy to have done so well in such a large class.

Chapter Seventeen

Nine of us crowded around Mrs. Nolly's dinner table, devouring platters of corn bread and chicken, bowls of summer squash and spinach, and tall glasses of milk. Flies beat against the window screens in an attempt to get at the good smells of Carver Coy's cooking.

"Not bad," said Mrs. Nolly, "except there's too much salt in the squash."

"It's hot weather," he said. "You always need a little extra in the summertime. How many times do I have to tell you about the Utah desert, woman?"

"Everybody had a good day, then, did they?" Clus, who always ate with his safari helmet on, was having some trouble keeping the chin strap out of the way of his fork. "Oh, Elizabeth, did I tell you I ran into Dr. Dickson a little while ago? He said to tell you that riding a horse over those big fences is not his idea of taking it easy for the rest of the summer. But he said congratulations, too."

"I know," I said, "I saw him."

"And so did I," said Carver. "He wanted to know if it was true that Mrs. Nolly was intending to keep riding with that arm broken the way it is."

"Of course I'm riding with my arm broken," Mrs. Nolly said. "I don't hold to the the saddle with my arms, Carver Coy, I hold with my legs."

Toby and the twins broke into giggles. When they caught each other's eyes, it started them giggling all over again.

Suzanne's thin little voice joined in, and even Clus got tickled at their carrying on.

"Good day at the shelter?" Rusty asked.

"Exceptional day," Clus beamed. "I couldn't have designed one myself that I'd like better, except I'm about to run out of pups. It's a little lonely down there. But — that's good. That's the whole point."

"I've got some news," Rusty said.

"Shoot," said Carver.

"They got Garson Gambill for drugging his horses."

"Where did you hear about that?" I wanted to know.

"Leroy Dailey was telling it down at the secretary's box this afternoon. They're going to announce the penalty at the opening of the show tomorrow."

Carver was lining things up in his mind. "That'll be one o'clock, it being Sunday."

Rusty went on. "He said Mr. Gambill didn't even blink an eye when the vets' reports came in. He said they couldn't touch him with a ten-foot pole . . . that he'd have his lawyer take action if they so much as mentioned his name, and like that."

"I knew they'd catch up to him. I knew he was into some funny business," Carver said. "I bet they gravel him good over this."

"It's encouraging to the rest of us that something can be done to root out people like him," Mrs. Nolly said. "When Major carries me into that ring tomorrow for the pleasure horse championship, I'll at least take heart that anything I might win comes honestly. And so can the rest of you, in your respective classes."

"I'm riding in the pleasure horse championship," Toby said sweetly.

"Of course you are, dear." Mrs. Nolly wrestled a piece of chicken around on the tines of her fork.

"Rusty, you couldn't have brought news that would have pleased me more," Clus said.

"Aye, I'm with you on that," Carver said.

"I feel sorry for Garson Gambill's horses," Suzanne said.

"Maybe he'll have to sell them," said one of the twins.

"Be just like him to figure a way to squirm out of this," Carver said bleakly. "It would be like him to do that."

"That's not all I heard," Rusty said. "The Daileys say Chicken turned them down on their offer for the Ragman."

Mrs. Nolly smiled. "Say something serious, Rusty."

"He just did," I said.

"Don't anybody breathe hard," said Carver, "or it'll knock me right over on the floor. What do you mean you turned them down? I thought you and the little spotted horse weren't on the best of terms. Look at all the money you could have had by selling him."

"They even added another thousand to the offer," I said.

Carver let loose a short high whistle on hearing that.

"You told them you wouldn't consider selling him, even for two thousand, five hundred dollars? What did they say? No, wait, don't tell me what Sidney said. Never much cared for him. Tell me what Leroy said."

"He wanted to know if I'd thought what it would mean to give up the chance to ride in international competition. All I could think of to say was that I was sorry. He wasn't very happy."

"I wish they'd ask me one time," Suzanne put in.

"Who doesn't?" said Mrs. Nolly. "This is pretty hard to understand."

"Good act," said Carver Coy. "All you've done is moan and groan over how much you were going to miss her — how things wouldn't be right without her. How you'd miss having the little horse jumping in the name of the Nolly Stable, and such as that."

"I thought you wanted a Thoroughbred like Eva's," Toby said.

"Everybody wants a Thoroughbred like Eva's," Rusty said.

I answered them all. "I thought that would make everything all right, but when I realized I would have enough money to buy a good horse, I realized I already had a good horse. Even if he did come in three colors."

"Mark one down for the Ragman," said Carver. "I knew he'd get the best of you."

"They say you aren't showing tomorrow." Rusty was really asking if it was true.

"I could have got us hurt today," I told him. "On the jump-off. It wasn't all that big a fence, but since I'd never schooled him over it, I was holding back on him too much. He knew something was wrong, but he did his best anyway. He made that jump all by himself, with no help from me."

"Aw, he could jump six feet and over," Clus said.

"All things considered, I'm relieved," said Carver. "I thought sure you'd leave us next year. Now I get to see the finishing touches put on the Ragman."

"And on the girl," said Uncle Clus. "She's got the butterfly spirit at last." He winked at me. "You know what that is?"

I smiled back, fluttering my fingers up and away from the table for him.

"You got it," he said. "You got it, all right."

Later, Carver tied his leather apron on and bent himself over one of King's troublesome hooves.

He said, "It's been a good ending to a good day, knowing you're going to stay with us, Elizabeth. Don't you worry. I'll take care of the Ragman for you this winter. You can come visit; work him out. And . . . when you have a free moment or two, I'd like to speak a few words to you about a little personal matter that's been weighing on my mind."

I didn't know what he meant by that. I only knew that the Ragman was waiting down the corridor for his feed. I pushed the heavy wheelbarrow up to his stall.

There he stood. And he seemed to be grinning at me.

Mrs. Nolly grinned all morning. It was an especially happy, sunny day, and the one she'd looked forward to. It soon would be time for the local pleasure horse championship, time for her and Big Boy's Major to show their stuff. Old-timers would drape themselves over fences and recall Major's prime as a top steeplechaser, and in the end, the two would ride away with the trophy, nodding to a polite, appreciative crowd.

"I've never seen a more lovely morning," she chortled. "Not ever. Where is Elizabeth, somebody?"

Seated on the floor, working his bridle with saddle soap, was Toby, who said, "Over there."

I was cleaning Mrs. Nolly's stirrups for her.

"Good morning," she said to me. "Dear, where is Toby?"

"Here," said Toby, looking up from the floor.

"I won't be worth a darn if I don't calm down, now will I?"

"It's a big day," I giggled. "In about half an hour, they'll be making that announcement about Garson Gambill."

"That's not what I'm so excited about. I'm wondering how the Major and I will look."

"I'm riding in the local pleasure horse class," Toby said sleepily.

"Of course, dear; I know, dear. That's what I wanted to talk to you about."

"Did I do something wrong?"

"Of course you didn't, did you, Toby? No, I wanted to talk to you about your little round face. Will it make you sensitive if I do that?"

"No ma'am, I guess not."

"When we have a very round face," she began delicately, "we have to pay special attention to our throat."

"Our throat?" Toby asked.

"It's this choker you've been wearing. Very smart indeed, and I like it. But I'd like it better if someone with a more angular face wore it. Do you get my point, Toby?"

"Not really," he said.

"The idea is not to attract attention to ourselves in the local pleasure horse competition. For instance, I would never dream of putting an expensive saddle on Major. I wouldn't wear my blue and green coat, either. Nor would I tie red bows into his mane. I want to be in good taste, you see.

"I keep my color ensemble very simple, along the lines of what you have on today. But I make sure I don't overemphasize my bad features, of which I have plenty. If I were you, I would wear a stock tie instead of a choker. It will lengthen your face."

I teased her. "That wasn't so hard, was it?"

"I don't have a stock tie," Toby said.

"You do now," and Mrs. Nolly pulled a fresh white one from her pocket.

"I don't have a stock pin," he said.

Mrs. Nolly pulled a gold fox head pin from her other pocket and peered over it at him. "This was my husband's, and I can tell you right now that it never failed to bring him good luck."

Toby was pleased. He held up the pin with his stubby fingers.

"Don't be late for your class, now. It's the first one today. And, Toby, I do want to tell you how glad I was when you won your very first ribbon. I hope you are very proud of what you've accomplished here."

What she meant was, "since you may not win another ribbon today."

But Toby simply blinked. He was bubbly with self-satisfaction.

"And perhaps I shouldn't compete against you children," she went on. "Perhaps at my age . . . with my disposition toward winning, and my long experience . . . perhaps I should just throw in the towel altogether. But you know it's my only vice. And I do get such a kick out of showing the old Major off. It's nice to keep a hand in — even if it is only one hand."

Toby studied the pin without comment. He'd never worn a good-luck charm before.

"I know you'll do well, Toby. It will be a great thrill just trying, won't it?"

"Yes ma'am." But what did she mean, just trying?

"And you aren't scared?"

"Oh no," Toby said, wide-eyed at the suggestion he might be. "No, ma'am, I'm going to win."

Mrs. Nolly chuckled with maternal understanding. "Of course, dear. Of course you are. You just do as I told you. Ride Stogy on a perfectly loose rein and fall in behind a horse you know you can trust to do right. Stogy will follow right along like a faithful old sheep dog, and you won't have to do a thing.

"And remember to smile, dear."

Toby tried two or three smiles, as if posing for a finicky photographer.

"The one with a little less tooth showing," she coached him. "There. There's the perfect smile for a pleasure horse class. It's a smile that says how happy you are just to be alive and aboard a horse, and that's going to count for a lot. The judge is going to pay attention when Toby goes riding by."

Toby suddenly reached his arms up and gave Mrs. Nolly a soft hug around the neck.

"You won't worry now, if for any reason the judge should overlook you," she said.

"I don't really think he thinks the judge will do that," I laughed.

"That's right, I don't," Toby said, all innocence and light. "But if he does, I promise to be a good sport, just like you would want me to be."

Mrs. Nolly smiled. "Why, with that attitude I wouldn't be surprised if you went out there and beat me. You're about as stubborn as three generations of Coys, once you've set your mind on something."

Little did she know.

Chapter Eighteen

"We have our hearts set on a very high goal," Leroy Dailey said into the microphone. It screeched after his last word; the sound engineer made some adjustments, then motioned for him to continue.

"It is the intention of the National Association of Exhibitors and Owners that no animal appearing in any of its shows be misused in any way whatever. Since the Highlands Charity Horse Show has the sanction of our organization, and has three of our executive members on its board of directors, we instructed our veterinarians to conduct tests to see whether stimulants or tranquilizing drugs have been used here.

"Three stables were checked yesterday. They were chosen by drawing and no irregularities were found. However, a fourth stable, the Garson Gambill Stable, was quite another matter. These reports I have in my hand testify to the fact that all six of the Gambill horses had been drugged.

"Three of them were tranquilized, according to our head veterinarian, and the other three were subjected to stimulative drugs. This kind of thing is unforgivable and reflects ill upon show people everywhere.

"Therefore, meeting in special session this morning, the board of directors of the Highlands Charity Horse Show drafted a resolution condemning the actions of Mr. Garson A. Gambill and/or his employees. The resolution calls, in part, for the return of all money and prizes he has won during the course of this show.

"His riders are forbidden to compete in today's championship class and it is the decision of our national association that no horse owned, ridden, or trained by Mr. Gambill may be shown in any show we sponsor for a period of ten years from today."

"That's the end of the Gambill Stables," Carver told me. We were all gathered at the gate, watching Dailey deliver his talk from the gazebo.

Mr. Dailey continued, "Our walking horse judge assures us he has kept complete notes on each class that has come before him, and will see to it that the other riders are awarded the trophies and ribbons in the correct order.

"It is also the decision of our organization that these actions be reported in full in our national magazine, which is subscribed to by hundreds of horse show secretaries in this country. This, we feel, will make it impossible for Mr. Gambill to continue his career in the show horse business, and will remove the blemish he has placed upon us this week in this beautiful mountain setting."

The announcer took the microphone and said, "We thank you, Mr. Dailey. We now ask that our local pleasure horses stand by. Class will proceed in ten minutes."

From behind us, Carver and I heard Garson Gambill yell, "Heads up!"

We turned to find him dashing toward the gate, his apricot habit, matching derby, and boots flashing in the sun. We ducked quickly and he sprang into the air, supporting his weight with one hand on the gate. He landed in the dust and raced on, skidding up to Leroy Dailey.

Mr. Dailey had just stepped out of the judges' stand into the sunlight when Gambill threatened him with his fist. Some of what Gambill was saying came through, but not enough to put together into sentences. Mrs. Nolly strained to hear, but it was impossible.

With Mr. Dailey standing still, Gambill ran little circles around him, growling and snapping over what he had said, squeaking in high-pitched tones about what he, Gambill, would do to get even.

Mr. Dailey, shrugging Gambill off, began walking. This only infuriated him more, and as they approached us, their voices began to come through clearly.

"I'll fix you, I'll fix you," Gambill squalled. "You'll pay, you'll pay."

"Nothing of the sort, my dear sir. You are the one who will pay. You are the one who mistreated your horses and collected prizes you had not won fairly."

Gambill danced up and down. "I don't want to go back to hanging wallpaper. It's all indoor work. I want to show horses for a living. Train and show!"

"I can appreciate a man's wanting to be out in the sunshine. But you alone are responsible for the clouds that hang over you today."

"You've arranged it so I'll have to sell all my horses. You are forcing me to give up the style of life I prefer."

"Pity," said Leroy Dailey. "Look what you've brought upon yourself."

Garson Gambill's cheeks flooded with tears. He said, "I will sue you for what you have done here today. I will get every nickel you earn for the rest of your life."

Mr. Dailey gazed off into the blue sky and said, "That will be quite a lot of nickels. I've been a very fortunate man, as I've often said. My family was not so well-to-do, but they gave me an education which enabled me to take up the practice of law, and I must say I've done rather well at it. And if I can entice you to invest your money in a lengthy law suit against me, nothing could please me more."

Leroy Dailey came through the gate, said hello all around, and went on. Garson Gambiil hopped along behind him, trying to think of something to say.

"Got you," I said as he passed. And Carver sighed: "I've never seen quite so beautiful a Sunday. It's a real tribute to summertime, a real tribute."

The sky was a high blue arc, the sun strong and sharp, the air breezy and clean.

Major's coat glistened and his tack was a dark mahogany. Mrs. Nolly was flawlessly turned out, from her jodhpur shoes and leggings right on up to the top of her soft hunt derby. She had chosen a gray linen coat and it set off her white hair nicely. Carver had dug around in a tack trunk and found her old aviator sunglasses. I had contributed a pair of tan gloves.

She was the perfect lady astride the perfect horse, the two so properly matched by weight and height that neither seemed too large or too small for the other. The only problem was her broken arm; it made her look somewhat unbalanced. And the heat was making it itch. But her serene, queenly smile never let on that anything was wrong, and when the gate opened and the class entered, she pushed the lean black gelding into a brisk trot.

The judge made a mark in his notebook. This did not go unnoticed and Mrs. Nolly chuckled and the big horse moved smoothly along.

When the class was in, Carver and I leaned on the gate with an assortment of old gentlemen who recalled Major's flamboyant youth, where he was shown, what he had won. "What a horse," Carver agreed.

"What a rider," I added.

"Aye, I was noticin'."

Suzanne was doing a better than average job of showing Jack, and Toby was true to his promise, letting the long thin filly pace herself to Major's every movement. Stogy was virtually a shadow to the big gelding.

Rusty was having a joyful ride on Spots, the dapple-gray mare, and for the fun of it, he had left his stirrups off. Spots trotted ahead and Rusty posted, knees in exactly the right place.

"Mrs. Nolly doesn't like him to do that," I told Carver. "She says it pulls the knees up too high on the horse, and she doesn't think it does a lot to develop a proper seat."

An old gent leaned around Carver and said, "The Australian Army does it." He was completely toothless. He gave me a wide black smile and turned his attention back to the class.

The twins were riding Peter and Prince shoulder to shoulder, sitting sloppily in the saddles, craning their heads around to see who was behind them, and talking to people in the box seats.

The judge put the horses through a walk, trot, and canter each way of the ring. It was a casual kind of competition, but one which Mrs. Nolly took in all seriousness. She had great respect for a horse who kept his head

166

together and responded to the gentlest touch of knee or hand. Major could even change gaits on voice command, he'd been at it so long.

"I swear it," Carver said. "She can say 'trot' and he'll trot."

"She says a stern expression on a rider's face can lose him a ribbon," I said.

"If the rider looks like he's having no fun, who's the judge to question it?"

Mrs. Nolly passed us, her lips turned up in an angelic smile, eyes straight ahead, a hearty "fiddle-faddle" slipping out the side of her mouth to show how confident she felt.

"It's all over and done," Carver called after her.

Toby was right behind her, the best of his three smiles pasted over his little round mouth. Mrs. Nolly was right about the stock tie.

A canter was called and Major stepped into stride. So did Stogy, and without the slightest help from Toby. It was monkey see, monkey do, and the judge was looking right at him. The judge let them take three more turns of the ring to see who was too fast, which riders were fighting their horses' mouths, which horses were switching their leads back and forth or showing irritability, and, hence, which would be the winners.

He'd seen enough. He called the horses onto the grass and went to each in turn, asking the rider to back his mount. When Major backed, Stogy did too, and the judge laughed over it, thinking Toby had signaled the filly early, maybe out of nervousness.

"That's all right, son," the judge said. He was finishing up his notes. He squinted up at Toby and gave him a smile. He said, "I must say I enjoyed seeing you ride in this class. I had the uncanny feeling that you were using mental telepathy of some kind. I don't think I saw any tension on those reins the whole time. And I watched closely, too."

The judge strode off and Mrs. Nolly nodded her head at Toby, winked, and nodded her head some more. "I bet anything you get a ribbon," she said to him.

"There are six prizes in this class," the announcer said, "and we will announce them in reverse order. Sixth place, Mr. Rusty Reinholt on Spots; fifth place goes to Michael Williams on Scat; fourth place and third place, Miss Debby Bledsoe on Prince, and Miss Betty Bledsoe on Peter."

Moms and dads and aunts and uncles shouted and clapped.

"Our second place goes — here we are — Miss Suzanne Greeley."

Mrs. Nolly felt a sudden pang for Toby, for the high hopes he'd had. The pang was a short one, though, for just then the announcer said, "And our first place ribbon and championship trophy go to number twelve."

Hearing a name and number called, Mrs. Nolly rode forward. It was her instinct. After all, she'd won the pleasure horse trophy so many times that she couldn't remember them all. But it was not her name and number that was called.

It was, "Number twelve, Master Toby Todson, on Stogy."

The Todson family and friends, who were perched in an upstairs box, let loose a combination of cheers and whistles.

"Look at him, he's numb," I told Carver. And without a horse to follow, Stogy went this way and that, not sure what Toby's jerks on the reins were supposed to mean. The pretty lady holding the trophy finally brought it to him, and when Stogy jogged out the gate, Toby nearly fell off.

Carver caught up the reins and I relieved Toby of the enormous trophy long enough for him to get down.

Toby mumbled, "I'm famous. Look at what I won."

"Aye," said Carver, "and look at what she didn't win."

Mrs. Nolly rode icily by, ignoring all of us.

"Don't worry about her," I said. "She's always a good sport."

Carver humphed at that. "She's always a good sport when she's winning, that's the catch."

"I just knew I would win something," Toby said.

"I just knew I would win," Mrs. Nolly moaned. "I always do, you see. It was in the bag, Carver said so."

"I thought you had a beautiful ride," I said.

"Where is Carver?"

"Downstairs, seeing to Major," I said.

Mrs. Nolly lay back on her cluttered studio couch, her panting dog Robo at her side. All the rosiness was gone from her face, and her eyes were very dull and heavy as they surveyed the room. Her dusty stereo produced its melancholy sounds, and she sipped from a glass of ice water. Robo whimpered, feeling her mood.

"That beautiful, beautiful song is 'Melody in F,' " she informed me. "It was written by Anton Rubinstein." She sighed. She listened a moment more. "He played before Chopin and Liszt, and it was Liszt who recommended that he finish his studies in Germany. There was a great story about Liszt, you know, when he fell hopelessly in love with a Russian princess. A sad movie was made about it.

"Anyway, this Rubinstein was a fabulous concert pianist, and he composed a great deal of music, even operas. Did I ever tell you my father was a piano teacher?"

I said yes. I asked if I could get her some more water.

"Well, I just want you to know I know a few things. I just want you to keep in mind that I am not an old fogy."

"Nobody thinks you are."

"Certain people evidently do," she said, leaving big spaces between the words. "Certain pleasure horse judges, for instance."

"But you said to be a good sport if you lose."

"Ahhhhhhhhhhhhhh-ha! That's just it. There are two kinds of losing. There is losing when you deserve to and losing when you don't deserve to. Mine is the second kind."

I felt like laughing, but Mrs. Nolly looked so pitiful and the music was so touching, I didn't dare.

"I could understand it if I could think of

a single thing that went wrong. But I can't, because nothing did, and I don't see how in the world I'm to learn from an experience like that."

"Maybe you'll win next year."

"I don't want to win *next* year. I want to win *this* year, like I was supposed to."

Outside, the hurry and bustle went on unabated. Hunters glided over fences, five-gaited horses racked around the ring, spectators came and went at the concession stand, and music was spliced between classes to entertain the crowd.

"I've got to go," I said. "It's almost time for the conformation hunters."

"You can't go and leave me on this cruelest of all cruel days, my dear."

"I have to." I gave Mrs. Nolly a kiss on the cheek and turned to leave.

"It's a conspiracy," Mrs. Nolly wailed. "Don't you let Carver Coy tease about this, because it's not funny."

Rubinstein's melody followed me down the stairs.

"How's she taking it?" Carver asked. "Not good. I can tell it in your face."

"She's awfully sad." I got Eva's saddle and bridle and headed down the corridor with Carver in tow. "Is she here yet?"

"Eva? Ah, she's been here for an hour, wandering about, smacking her boots with her crop and complaining that Spots will fall down over the first fence."

"Sounds just like her."

"Well, I'll be out front. I want to see how she reacts. Good, I bet."

Rusty was already astride Beau and ready for his class to be called. Eva stood beside him, chatting aimlessly about assorted things, throwing out criticisms of every horse that passed.

"You ought not be so callous," said Carver. "Just think of it the other way around. It's not so pleasant then."

"On top of it all," Eva replied, "I have to ride that broken-down old mare."

Carver said, "I don't think you will, after all." On cue I led Eva's fine hunter out of the barn and into the sun.

"It's Garry!" Eva said. "I don't believe this, he's not lame."

"Aye. Sound as he can be."

"Sound enough to ride in conformation hunter today?"

"As a surprise," Rusty told her.

"And what's Jiggsie doing with him, I'd like to know?"

That split it with Carver.

"What Jiggsie has been doing all this week — besides doing a splendid job of showing the Ragman — is making this horse sound so you could ride him. Which hasn't done her a whole lot of good, what with her getting over pneumonia and having to stay late doing extra chores on account of Mrs. Nolly's arm being broken. Hush, Rusty, I'm not done."

Carver's face was flushed in fury.

"You went off in that blasted creek and lamed up a good horse after you'd been told repeatedly not to run him in there. So every day and night, while you've been off Lord-knows-where, Elizabeth has been wrapping that hoof in poultices, soaking out the bruise. And every time the poultice would come off, she'd put it right back on, and never complained. And kept him on a diet of bran mash, which was just that much more for her to see to.

"And about got herself worn out attending to your horse, which is what you should have been doing, instead of sitting around pouting about it. And why she bothered, except for the love of good horseflesh and pity for the likes of you, I can't imagine. But she did, and she was glad to, and that's what Jiggsie has been up to!"

Carver turned and strode off into the barn.

Eva jerked the reins out of my hands, sprang into the saddle, and rode off just as angrily.

"Good try," Rusty said. "I should have figured she would take it like that."

Through the upstairs window, Mrs. Nolly's favorite melody drifted like thin smoke. I now knew just how she felt.

The hunter judges decided upon special workouts for the top twelve conformation hunters. It had been a long, tiring class, in the course of which the sun brightened and grew hotter. The shade under the trees was still a dense, mid-summer black and was highly prized by spectators.

Carver, Rusty, and I sat watching Eva put William Tell through his paces. First he popped over eight hunt course fences, stopped and backed at the water hazard, then completed a figure eight at a trot. The second figure eight he took at an easy canter. He was satiny and sleek from hours of grooming by none other than Chicken Jiggsen.

"She sure knows how to ride." I had to give her that.

"Yeah," said Carver, "and there's times

when I think I could actually wring her neck. No, I take it back. But sometimes I want to."

"That's the kind of horse you wanted," Rusty said.

"To a T." I watched him, still a little wistful.

"He's perfect," Carver said. "Not too much of him, not too little — just the right amount."

Eva finished the routine without error, dismounted, and led William Tell over to a group of admirers seated by the fence.

When Rusty's turn came, Beau moved over the course in fine fashion, backed just right, and took his figure eights nearly as well as Eva's horse had. Six of the entries, Rusty and Eva among them, then were called to the ring to show on the "flat."

The judges watched them walk for a few minutes before ordering a gallop. The hunters stretched to their full length, gobbling up yards of ground with each stride.

"Halt!" called the announcer. William Tell practically sat down in the dust, and Beau was right with him. The judges marked their ballots and talked among themselves. Carver shaded his eyes, the better to see from the gate.

The same old gent was there, and when he recognized me, he said, "They also used to post without stirrups in the German Cavalry."

"It'll be an easy choice," Carver said. "I could nearly place them myself."

"I'd put Rusty second," I said, and it so happened the judges did, too. Rusty rode up to us with a long red ribbon and a grateful grin.

And Eva, predictably enough, won first. But no one could have anticipated what she was about to do when she rode up to me and gave me a hard stare. She simply handed down her trophy.

"Here," she said. "You earned this. I'm sorry for the things I said — about you, and about your horse." I took the trophy hesitantly. Eva threaded through the crowd, heading for the barn.

"Bless be," said Carver. "Now you've won something worth winning."

And only I could anticipate what Carver was about to do.

"That matter I discussed with you. I think it's time. You wait for me, now, don't get gone anywhere. If things don't go my way, I'll need plenty of bucking up."

A long time passed. The ring was cleared and the jump crew put to work. Playing over and over, Melody in F clashed with a bouncy waltz the announcer had chosen. It blared through the loudspeakers as I watched Judge Carsells' championship jump course take form.

Finally, Carver came ambling down the stairs from the kitchen of Mrs. Nolly's apartment.

"Well," he said, squinting the sun from his eyes and gazing out over the show ground. "I decided to ask Mrs. Nolly if she would be my wife, but in the end, when it came right down to it, I couldn't do it," he said dejectedly.

"But I did it anyway, and she said yes to me."

Carver wrapped me in a bear hug and swung me around.

"I just didn't want you people to think I was a washed-up old fogy," he said.

Upstairs, Mrs. Nolly changed her tune. The new record was of banjo music, and Mrs. Nolly was singing, "Yes sir, that's my baby; no sir, I don't mean maybe; yes sir, that's my baby now."

Chapter Nineteen

As the day grew hotter, the horses lathered. No breeze stirred. Spectators carrying umbrellas against the sun had to be reminded repeatedly to stay away from the edge of the ring.

The announcer was ruffled when he said, "Lady with the pink umbrella — please, please, please." A pink mushroom finally folded and was put away.

From the entrance to the park, the show ground below was a patchwork quilt of striped awnings and banners, gaily painted vans and trailers, cars and horses, people coming and going, taking care of chores and finding the best vantage points from which to see the remaining classes.

I watched for a long time, catching bits and pieces of announcements, feeling the sun beat down. Ahead lay the trail on which the Ragman had received most of his training just a few weeks before. "Not every horse is a natural," I remembered Carver saying. "It wouldn't do you any harm to just pretend like he existed or something."

I patted the Ragman and he jogged into the edge of the silent, cool woods. The floor of the forest was mossy and damp, the bark of the trees heavy with a pale green lichen, and the clearings thick with fluffy white snakeroot that swayed in an eerie way.

A lot of the trail was downhill and slippery. There were springs to jump and the trunks of huge fallen trees, and it ended at the pinnacle of the hunt field. The sweet, nutty aroma of rotting logs scented the air and the Ragman went on, judging the distance to a giant oak trunk.

"Up, boy!" I whispered along his neck, and the Ragman sprang with all his might. Even Major could not go as high; even Beau had met his match in the pinto.

The Dailey brothers didn't give up all that easily. They put Rusty on Wampum — surprise of all surprises — and he won the third-place ribbon behind Sally Merriwell's champion gray. They even made him the same offer about taking the show circuit with them.

"It's remarkable what that boy can do with that mare," said Leroy Dailey.

"Never saw anything to beat it," said the proud bride-to-be, showing off the double horseshoe nails Carver had given her for an engagement ring. And Carver was all flustered and rosy-cheeked as news of his coming marriage spread among his friends.

You should have seen Clus. He'd found homes for almost all of the luckless dogs at the animal shelter; and he'd banked over a thousand dollars to start a public education program in the fall.

Mother caught art show fever and was no longer so worried about me "riding those big horses over those big jumps." She figured I could take care of myself by now, and, moreover, she could take care of herself, too. She painted up a storm, getting ready for the upcoming city art show.

Dad confided that he had thought I'd never forgive him for giving me the Ragman. "I knew enough about horses from my boyhood to know he wasn't much, on the surface. But it was all the money I had, and that's how you came by him."

Toby bought a huge picture of himself with the championship pleasure horse trophy; Mrs. Nolly still turned her head away whenever she passed it, never guessing it was her broken arm that bothered the judge. "It just plain sets a bad example for you young people," the judge told me later. "People who are sick or hurt ought to be in a sick bed, not in a show ring."

The walls of the tack room were covered with ribbons, and trophies were set here and there among the saddles and bridles spread across the floor. Much to my surprise, not only was Toby soaping and polishing the leather, Eva was. She arrived that afternoon wearing old jeans, a worn-out shirt of her father's, and a pair of sneakers with holes in the toes. In an hour or two, she looked just like me: arms and face grimy from the work, hair flecked with hay and straw.

And she wanted me to help keep William Tell in shape. "To tell you the truth, Elizabeth, I could use a few friends. I can't use any more enemies." Whatever became of Jiggsie Jiggsen, I wondered?

Rusty made his decision to stay with the hard-working Nolly Stables, "and help you take care of the Ragman." He turned red every time he talked to me, and I couldn't figure what changed him. Probably my success with a woolly, glass-eyed little horse.

The kids got together and gave me the first piece of equipment I ever owned, a deluxe show halter with brass fittings. The name plate said MR. RAGMAN, THE BEST. Suzanne did the honors, and the twins started giggling. Of course, anything set them off these days.

I didn't see Rusty again that day, but he left me this note: "Dear Elizabeth — Don't forget the horse show ball. I'll pick you up at seven tonight. — Charles." Added in parentheses was "Rusty."

The Ragman got a special treat, a long run in the grazing pasture. He kicked up at gangs of butterflies flitting happily about, galloped around for a bit, then rolled in the dust to scratch his back. He was a mess, and I marked down just one more chore to do. He shook himself, rolled his eyes, and sneezed. At me, it seemed.

I was sunning on my favorite rock up by the hunt course when they called the walking horses into the ring. The familiar music began, and the crowd started its hooting and clapping. I sat up to take a look, wondering who was left now that Garson Gambill was out of the way.

There was a whole ring full of horses, and much to my amazement, Carver Coy was right in the thick of it. At every turn of the ring, he tipped his hat, the grandstand went wild, Benny flashed along in the finest fettle, and when the wind caught in Carver's coat-tails, the red satin shone in the sun.

And nobody, but nobody, ever called me Chicken again.